OCCULT

By

Laura Siobhân Croft

TELEMACHUS PRESS

Cover art and design by Laura Croft

Scene separators ©Dreamstime_2370365

Published by Telemachus Press, LLC
http://www.telemachuspress.com

ISBN: 978-1-942899-94-5 (Paperback)

Version 2016.11.02

10 9 8 7 6 5 4 3 2 1

Table of Contents

OCCULT

Publisher's note:
This book follows punctuation and
spelling rules of the UK,
the author's home country.

Chapter One

A New Beginning

THE FULL MOON shone eerily in the night sky. All was quiet except for the shuffling of six feet as three figures crept slowly in the darkness. They were making their way towards a tall, old-looking house which had arch-shaped windows made of black iron and was situated on the hillside.

The wind howled as the three figures made their way, up the path and towards the entrance of the house.

One of them pulled out a small, silver key from their pocket and placed it into the keyhole and slowly turned it until it gave a small *"click!"*

The wooden door opened and the figures stood in the doorway and looked inside into the darkness and emptiness of the house.

They entered the room and quietly shut the door behind them. The figures walked across a viridian green carpet towards a large wooden staircase. Slowly they climbed and stopped at the top of the landing and eyed the wooden door that was in front of them and waited nervously.

Two of the figures turned towards each other, they couldn't keep it in any longer, and giggled at the thought of what they were about to do.

The moon shone through one of the windows, which illuminated the figures who were in fact three young teenage boys.

"Would you be quiet, he'll hear you!" one of the boys said warning his friends. He was tall and had brown eyes and blond floppy hair and was smartly dressed in a pale blue long-sleeved shirt and dark blue jeans.

"Sorry Jon!", apologised one of the other boys. He had blue eyes, short, curly, ginger hair and freckles and was called Danny Murray and wore a red and black T-shirt and black jeans and had a silver hoop earring in his left ear.

"And I wish you would stop calling me that! My name is *Jonathan!*"

"Oh come on!" Danny said with a grin. "Be cool man!"

"I *am* cool!" Jonathan said getting annoyed. "I'm just saying I would prefer it if you called me by my full name, that's all!"

"Just chill man, would ya'!" Danny said rolling his eyes.

Jonathan looked at his friends. "Sorry", he said. "I guess I'm just a little nervous of how he's gonna take it. You know what James is like if he's in one of his moods, he's not gonna like it y'know!"

Danny looked at Jonathan and reminded him of when it had been their birthdays. "Yeah well, he should be expecting it shouldn't he, after all he bombed you with water balloons on *your* birthday, put cake in my face on mine...and as for Drew here", he said putting his hand on the other boy's shoulder; "he sprayed him with cream!"

"Yes! But can we please stop these birthday pranks now?" Jonathan asked. "We're *thirteen*, it's time to grow up!"

Danny grinned. "Yeah, but that doesn't mean we have to become boring!"

Jonathan was about to reply when Drew suddenly spoke. "Er guys, I think he's up".

His voice was gentle and he had green eyes and light brown floppy hair with dark streaks. He had a cute looking face and was dressed in a light grey hooded top, black T-shirt and indigo coloured jeans.

"Alright!" Danny said with a twinkle in his eye, "Let's get this party started!" The three boys waited nervously for the wooden door in front of them to open.

Jonathan stepped back whilst the other two prepared themselves for the prank they were about to commit.

Slowly the door opened and out stepped a tall, dark haired boy, with bright blue eyes who was still half-asleep and wearing a black vest top and red boxer shorts.

"HAPPY BIRTHDAY!" yelled Danny as he and Drew sprayed different colours of silly string at him. James woke at the sound of their voices and began to shield his face with his muscled arms, but it was too late. He was covered.

Suddenly they heard a voice speak out, "What is going on out there!?" They watched as another door opened and out stepped James's Mum wearing a long pink nightie and looking quite tired. She had brown eyes and short brown hair in a bob.

"Oh my God! What have you done to him!?" she asked as she looked at her son. She clearly wasn't happy and neither was James.

"Sorry Mrs Darson", Jonathan apologised. "I did tell them *not* to do it!" He glared at the other two.

"If I had known what you were planning to do I would never have let you borrow the key!" Mrs Darson said as she put her hands on her hips and looked at Danny and Drew who quickly apologised.

"Sorry Mrs Darson", they said in a quiet whisper and then looked down at the floor.

Mrs Darson shook her head and sighed. "James, get that stuff off you and go back to bed", she told her son, "that goes for the rest of you, in the spare room, your beds are made. Now please I don't want to hear any more disturbances. Goodnight", and she turned away and went back into her room.

James looked sternly at his so-called friends and then walked into the bathroom slamming the door behind him.

"See, I told you he wouldn't like it", Jonathan said, frowning at the other two who were looking pretty sorry for themselves. "Just go to bed ok and I'll talk to him".

Danny and Drew nodded and then turned away and walked down the corridor towards the door at the end as Jonathan walked up to the bathroom door and tried to make amends with James.

"James? Are you ok?" he asked, there was no reply. "Listen, I told them not to do it. It was Danny's idea and he's sorry, it won't happen again. It's over, ok? James? We're still cool aren't we? James?"

"Get Lost!" came James's reply through the door.

"Ok then, I'll go", Jonathan said as he turned away. "Just don't hate them. These birthday pranks are over, no more. Sorry James. Goodnight then". He headed towards the door at the end of the corridor and could hear the other two getting ready for bed.

"He's not happy y'know", he told them as he entered the room.

"I'm sorry ok", Danny said. "He'll cheer up tomorrow when he sees what I've got him for his birthday won't he? Well?"

"I hope so", replied Jonathan. "Goodnight guys".

"Nite".

"Happy Birthday darling!" Mrs Darson said the next day as she handed her son a card. She was smartly dressed in a knee-length black skirt and a pink top and wore matching pearl bracelet, necklace and earrings.

James took the card, "Cheers!", he said. He was wearing a black vest top, faded blue denim jeans and a beige jacket and his hair was all gelled up at the front.

"Yeah! Happy Birthday dude!", Danny said smiling as he, Jonathan and Drew entered the lounge wearing the same clothes as they had on the previous night.

"Thanks", James replied looking away, he still hadn't forgiven him for what he and Drew had done.

"Hey so no hard feelings about last night then? No?" Danny asked him hopefully. "No", James said still looking away and still not happy. Suddenly James felt an arm around his neck and a hand rested on his shoulder. He turned and saw Danny's face grinning at him.

"Great!", Danny said. "Wait 'til you see what we've got in store for you!"

James looked nervously at his friend; he didn't like the sound of that and neither did his mother.

"Now I don't want you guys getting into any mischief", she told them, "and I want you to stay safe, ok?"

"Don't worry Mrs Darson", Jonathan reassured her, "*I'll* make sure they stay out of trouble". Jonathan was the eldest of the four friends and saw it as his responsibility to be the one in charge of the others and to make sure they behaved themselves.

Mrs Darson smiled and then went into the kitchen and made them all some marmalade on toast for breakfast and a glass of orange juice whilst the others watched James open his cards.

After they had eaten breakfast the four boys gathered in the hallway where Mrs Darson spoke to them once again. "Now I want you all to promise me you'll stay safe and not get up to any mischief. I want you back at this house just before midnight. Is that understood?"

Jonathan looked confused, *"Midnight!?"* he said. "Are you sure Mrs Darson? That's a bit late isn't it?"

"Jon, shut up!", Danny said frowning at him.

"Absolutely sure", Mrs Darson said, "it may be James's birthday but we have a surprise for you all!"

"A surprise? For *all* of us!? Wow, what is it?" Danny asked.

"You will find out tonight, when all will be revealed", she replied, "now go and have fun and enjoy yourselves and take care".

The boys turned around and headed down the long corridor towards the wooden door as Mrs Darson watched them leave. "This is gonna come as a shock to them Harry", she said as her husband came down the stairs. He had light brown scruffy hair and a beard and was wearing a dark blue dressing gown which matched his eyes.

"I know dear, but it's time they learnt the *truth* about themselves". His voice was deep and a little husky.

"I know", Mrs Darson said looking down at the floor, "I just wish they could stay *normal*!"

Mr Darson put his arm around her neck and rested his hand on her right shoulder. "They must know the *truth* Rachel", he said, "and if Julia's right about the prophecy then they could be the ones to change it all! Now come on, we have to get the things ready for tonight and call the others". He turned away not noticing the tears in his wife's eyes.

"Ok…open them!" Danny said as he took his hands away from James's eyes. They had led him to a secret location and James couldn't believe it when he looked out onto the muddy track where the car rallies were held.

"Wow!" he said as he stared open mouthed at one of the cars that sped by them. It was a bright red sports car with yellow lightning effects on the side and bonnet.

"Happy Birthday dude!" Danny said smiling as he noticed James's expression.

"But how did you…"

"My Dad knows one of the guys who works here and owes my Dad a favour", Danny told him.

Suddenly the two cars that had been racing around on the track pulled up in front of the four friends and two men stepped out of the vehicles. One was a tall, bald-headed guy with stubble and dressed in black and was the driver of the blue and purple sports car and the other was a tall, clean-shaven guy with shoulder-length wavy hair and dressed in red. He was the driver of the red sports car and waved as he noticed the boys.

"Danny hi!", he said smiling. "Right let's get you kids kitted up shall we?"

"Hi Matt!", Danny replied waving back. "Yeah let's do this!"

A few minutes later all the boys, except for Jonathan were all ready to go for a ride in the two cars. Danny and Drew went with Matt and James went with the other guy who was called Steve.

Jonathan watched from the sidelines, this wasn't his kind of thing but he kept his eyes fixed on the cars and held his breath as they sped by in a blur of colour and did some sharp turns, spraying mud into the air.

"Wow!", James said smiling. "That was so cool!"

"You liked that then!?" Steve said surprised. "Well let's go a bit faster alright? Hold on!" He quickly did a sharp turn and sped off in the opposite direction as the other car did a few spins in the mud.

"That was awesome dude!" Danny said smiling at Matt; it was like being on a fast ride at the fairground.

"Pleased you liked it!" Matt replied smiling back; "hey you ok in the back?"

"Uh-huh!", came a small voice from the back seat.

Danny turned around. "Hey dude, you don't look so good!" he said as he noticed Drew's face turning a pale shade of green.

"Hey no hurling in this car!" Matt warned him. "Let's get you out". He slowly put his foot on the brake so as not to upset Drew's stomach any more and very slowly the car came to a stand still and Drew got out.

"So we'll catch you later then!" Danny told him as he followed him out of the car.

"Uh-huh", Drew nodded as he removed his helmet. He walked over to where Jonathan was watching from the sidelines with his helmet under his arm.

"You couldn't handle the speed then?" Jonathan asked as Drew approached him.

"No", Drew replied and then walked away to get changed, he didn't feel very comfortable in tight, white Lycra.

"So", Matt said as Danny got back in the car, "I bet it came as a shock to you when your parents told ya', but don't worry you'll get used to it".

Danny looked at him, "Told me what?" he asked.

Matt smiled. "You don't have to pretend Danny, I know and as you're all thirteen now, you and your friends, they must have told you, but don't know why they didn't tell you as individuals. They probably wanted you to go through this together. So what *are* your friends? Are you the same or *different*?"

Danny stared at Matt. "What are you talking about, Matt?"

Matt glanced at Danny. "Your parents *have* told you, haven't they? The *truth*? Your *destiny*?"

"My *destiny*!?" Danny repeated, still having no idea what Matt was talking about; "they haven't told me anything! What do you mean the *truth*?"

Matt looked stern as he focused on the track and took the car for another spin, "Look, just forget it ok, I thought they would have told you, sorry".

"Told me *what* Matt?" Danny was getting anxious now as he stared at Matt trying to get him to reveal what he knew.

"It's nothing ok, so just drop it!" Matt replied in an irritated tone.

Danny sat there quietly and thought to himself no longer interested in the car ride. What is he talking about? Does he know something that I don't? What does he mean my *destiny?* When I get home I'm gonna demand some answers!

Matt was also thinking to himself. I can't believe I almost told him! *Why* doesn't he know yet? Are they planning on him to live a *lie!?*

After the boys had finished at the track they headed off to *Pasta Palace* where they decided to have a meal.

It was a large restaurant, which was very cosy and fancy inside, and had large round mustard coloured tables and chairs and a purple carpet.

"Ok, so James, Drew's gonna pay your share ok?" Jonathan said as they took a seat at one of the tables and looked at the bright red menus that were laid out on top.

"Cool", James said not looking up. He had taken a seat next to Jonathan, and Danny was opposite, next to Drew.

Jonathan noticed that Danny wasn't his usual happy and hyper self and had been like that since he left the track. Something was wrong.

"Hey Danny, are you ok?" he asked. "You've looked like a zombie ever since you got out that car! Has something happened?"

The others looked at him waiting for an answer.

"I can't stop thinking about what Matt said to me...or what he *didn't* say", Danny replied as he frowned at the carpet.

"What do you mean Danny?" Jonathan said looking at him confused.

Danny told them what Matt had said. "Well, he said that my parents should have told me something today. He also asked me *what* you guys *were* and if we were the *same*!"

They stared at him. "What we *were*!?" James asked bewildered. "What did he mean by that?"

Jonathan thought he had the answer but it sounded stupid but said it anyway. "Is he saying… we're *not* human!?"

James put his hands up like claws and squinted his eyes, "Yeah we're all mutants! Grrrrrrrrrrrr!"

Jonathan and Drew found this hilarious and burst out laughing along with James as Danny stared at them open mouthed and then he started laughing too as he realised that this was a silly explanation.

"Yeah, you're right!" he smiled. "I mean it's Matt, you can't take him seriously! He's just trying to freak me out!"

Suddenly they heard a soft, gentle voice addressing them. Jonathan turned round and saw a young, pretty girl who had long blond hair tied back into a ponytail. She was dressed in a light purple and silver uniform and holding a pen and notepad in her hands. Her name badge said *Gabriella*.

"Hello boys, what can I get ya'?" She asked smiling.

"Hello", Jonathan said smiling back. "Er yeah I think we're ready to order", he looked at the others, "should we have a starter guys?"

"Yeah!" Danny grinned. "Let's have garlic bread!"

"I don't like garlic", James said as he looked at Danny.

"Since when!?" Danny asked slightly annoyed.

"Since always!" James told him.

Jonathan could see that this was going to cause an argument so decided against it, it was James's birthday after all and they would only have what James wanted.

"Ok so we won't have garlic bread, or any starter", he told the waitress, "just the buffet thanks".

Gabriella noted this down and then asked them what they would like to drink.

"Can we have four Pepsi's please?" Jonathan asked.

"Yeah sure", Gabriella replied smiling, "just help yourselves to the buffet, the plates are around the corner and I'll bring your drinks over, ok. Thank you boys".

She left as Danny started on James again, "So why don't you like garlic?"

"I just don't ok!" James snapped. He was beginning to get very irritated and Jonathan could sense this and quickly intervened before it got out of hand.

"Look, it doesn't matter if he likes garlic or not", he said looking across at Danny who was still frowning. "Let's just have our meal and then move on to the next birthday treat".

"Which is?" James asked looking at him curiously.

"Well...", Jonathan started to smile, "do you know that film you wanted to see..."

Chapter Two
The Vision

AFTER THEY HAD eaten they went to the cinema and took their seats in the front row and stared at the huge bloodied up letters on the big black screen, *Voodoo* it read. "Thanks Jonathan", James said as he took a seat next to him, "But ya' do know that this is an *eighteen*!?"

"Yeah I know", Jonathan replied staring at the screen.

James was surprised, "So...we *shouldn't* really be watching this film!" He looked at him wondering why Jonathan was breaking the law. It just wasn't like him.

"Since when did you care about rules!?" Jonathan turned to look at him, frowning.

"I *don't* but you *do*!"

"Yeah well you really wanted to see this film, and it's your birthday so I'll bend the rules just this *once*". They both put their heads down knowing that this was wrong.

"Are you *sure* that we're not gonna get caught?" James asked worryingly.

Jonathan got up from his seat and looked at the empty chairs around them. "I doubt it", he said, "there is no one else here!"

Danny looked at them then with a suspicious look on his face, "And we *didn't* get ID'd!" He exclaimed. "Isn't that *weird*!"

Jonathan turned and looked at him then frowning, "That is weird yes. Normally they check. I told one of the guys here, Tobey, that we wanted to see this film and he said that he would have a word with his boss so that we wouldn't get ID'd! I'm quite curious to learn *how* he did that!"

"Who cares! Let's just enjoy the film, now sit down would ya'!" Danny told him as the lights went down and the film began to play. Jonathan took his seat between Danny and James as the title began to change. *How well do you really know your friends?* it said.

A while into the film, Jonathan, James and Danny were getting really into it and gazed open mouthed at the screen and didn't realise that Drew had closed his eyes trying to block out the horror, not interested in it at all like his friends.

Suddenly they all jumped out of their seats in horror as Drew gave out a blood-curdling scream…

"NOOOOOOOOOOOOOOOOOOOOOOOOOOOOOOOO OOOOOOOOOOO!!!"

"What the…?" James said angrily as he stared in Drew's direction.

"Dude! Are you *trying* to scare us to death!?" Danny looked at him frowning as Drew sat there looking down at the floor with a worried expression on his face.

"I…I…", he stuttered, "…I'm sorry, I…I can't do this!" And he got out of his seat and ran out of the screening room as the others stared after him curiously.

"What's eating him!?" wondered James.

"I'll go", Jonathan decided, "you guys stay here and watch the rest of the film, ok?" And with that he walked out of the screening room and went to find Drew as the other two looked at each other and then at the doors suspiciously.

There was no one else around when Jonathan entered the main foyer and found Drew facing the wall in one of the corners and crying his heart out.

"It happened again, didn't it!?" he said as he walked over to him. "This has to stop Drew. We're friends. There shouldn't be secrets amongst us. You've got to tell them".

"Tell us *what*!?"

Jonathan turned around and saw that James and Danny had followed him out.

"I thought I told you to stay and watch the film!" Jonathan told them, he was a bit annoyed.

"Yeah well we want to know what's going on!" James replied as he and Danny walked over to Jonathan.

"Yeah dude, why'd ya' freak out like that!?" Danny asked looking across at Drew with a concerned look on his face. He didn't like to see Drew upset.

Jonathan looked over at him, he had his back turned and stood quietly in the corner. "Drew, you're gonna have to tell them", Jonathan said. "If you don't then I will!"

"I can't", Drew replied in a quiet whisper. They could hear the pain in his voice.

"Then I'm sorry", Jonathan was about to tell James and Danny what was causing the upset when Drew slowly turned around and looked at Jonathan, tears were streaming from his eyes as he pleaded with him not to tell them.

James was starting to get a bit agitated. "If ya', *don't* tell me then I'll *make* ya' tell me!" he threatened holding up his fist.

Jonathan frowned at him. He had no choice. He was going to have to tell them despite Drew staring at him in horror.

Jonathan took a deep breath, "Ok; well it all started after Drew's birthday. He told me he kept on having these dreams, well more like nightmares and it was the same thing over and over nearly every night".

"What kind of thing?" James asked angrily.

"Well", Jonathan continued, "they're about us, but not us now; we're different, older. We're in this dark place and there's this lightning, *red* lightning and…and it's coming towards you James! And then… well…" he stopped.

James went up to him, "And then *what*!?" he demanded.

"Well…" Jonathan looked away reluctant to tell him what happened next as he knew that if James found out he wouldn't be happy about it but with James standing so close and breathing down his neck he revealed the truth.

"You burst into flames!"

"What!?" James glared at him angrily and couldn't believe what he had just heard.

"But we don't know what it means, and…" Jonathan quickly tried to calm him down but it was no good James's temper got the better of him.

"I'll tell ya' what it means, *he* wants to see me *dead*!" His tone was fierce as he stared across at Drew.

"No!" he cried out.

"No it doesn't!" Jonathan told him but James wasn't listening.

"*Yes* it does!" he said turning back and frowning angrily at Jonathan. "He's *never* liked me! and what are *you* doing in this dream?"

Jonathan couldn't answer. Truthfully he didn't know as Drew had only seen James in his dream being set on fire and didn't know if he and the others had tried to help or what happened next as Drew had always woken up screaming at that point. He just turned his head and looked down at the floor.

"Humph! Well thanks a lot!" James snapped. "Some friends *you* are!" He had had enough and ran out of the door and Jonathan looked and called after him.

Drew started to cry again.

"Oh no!" Jonathan sighed turning his head. "You stay here and I'll go and talk to James".

"Ok", Danny agreed.

Jonathan went outside determined to fix this mess and found James standing with his fists clenched at the bottom of the stone steps.

"Stay away from me Jonathan or I might use you as a punching bag!" He warned as he heard Jonathan approaching.

"C'mon James, it doesn't mean anything", Jonathan told him. "This is really *upsetting* Drew!"

"*He's* upset!?" James turned to look at him; "*I'm* the one being set on fire!"

Jonathan could see that this wasn't going to be easy. "It *doesn't* mean anything", he tried to tell him, "it's just a stupid dream James! It's not like it's gonna happen! Come on we can't let this thing get in the way and affect our friendship!"

"*Friends* aren't supposed to have dreams that their *friend* is being set on fire!" James snarled.

"It *doesn't* mean that's gonna happen James!" Jonathan repeated, he clearly wasn't listening. "Dreams have hidden meanings".

"So what's it *mean*?"

"I don't know, but I do know that Drew doesn't hate you James", he said as he carefully placed his hand upon his friend's right shoulder. "C'mon let's go back in and watch the rest of the film, and let Drew know you're ok with him". Jonathan was prepared for James to shove his hand away but instead James just agreed and had suddenly become very calm.

Jonathan removed his hand and they turned around and walked back up the steps and into the cinema. Danny turned to look at them as they entered the foyer and Jonathan gave him a thumbs up to let him know everything was alright. James didn't say anything, ignoring them as he walked past and into the screening room again.

Jonathan and Danny looked at each other and followed not saying anything as they closed the door behind them.

Drew decided not to watch the film and sat quietly in the foyer, wiping the tears away from his eyes as he waited patiently for his friends to return.

Later that night the four boys got changed and went into one of the nightclubs in town. Jonathan was wearing a short-sleeved white shirt with a green tie and black trousers and Danny was dressed in a funky purple and yellow T-shirt with blue jeans. They were laughing away as they danced to the music as Drew sat on his own watching them from the bright pink sofas in the seating area. He was wearing a black T-shirt and a blue and white striped tracksuit combo.

"C'mon dude, get up and dance!" Danny encouraged him as he looked across and smiled.

Different coloured strobe lighting lit up the dance floor and James walked over from the bar, drink in hand, a smirk on his face and dressed in a black vest top and jeans.

"Is he still upset about those *stupid* dreams!?" he grinned. "And *why me*? Well I'll tell ya' why…it's because he's *jealous*! He's always been jealous of my *good looks*! And *that* is why he wants to see me *dead*!"

He took a swig of his drink as the others looked at him. Jonathan frowned. "Are you *drunk*!?" he asked. "Is that *alcohol*!?"

"So what if it is!" James teased; "we've already broken one rule today!"

Jonathan stared at him, "Well that was wrong, *very* wrong! And I regret it", he told him; "you *shouldn't* break the law James! Anyway *no one* here should be given alcohol; it's an *underage* club!"

"Chick at the bar gave it to me", James grinned, looking at Danny, "called me *special!* Think she wants me!"

Danny looked across at the bar and grinned also, "Hate to break it to ya' dude, but she's hooked up!"

James, Jonathan and Drew looked over and saw the barmaid; a dark-skinned beauty with black curly hair and dressed in yellow, kissing a tall handsome, brown-haired guy dressed in black.

"The b…!" James started but Jonathan interrupted as he recognised the guy as Tobey from the cinema, the one who had got them to see that film. Jonathan had some questions he wanted answered and walked over towards Tobey as he called his name and the others followed.

Tobey heard his name being called and turned around as Jonathan came over. "Hey! Jonathan Jones!" he said smiling. "What can I do for ya'?"

"I would like to ask *how* you got us in to see that film without being ID'd?" he said looking up at him.

Tobey looked at him for a moment and then the top corner of his mouth went up and his eyes twinkled. He raised his hands and wiggled his fingers as if he were casting a spell. "Magic!" he smiled.

"No seriously, *how*?" Jonathan wasn't amused.

Tobey winked and smiled again, "Like I said, *magic!*" He turned towards his girlfriend, "See ya' later Bonnie", he said with a glint in his eye. She smiled as he walked away and took her place back behind the bar.

"Hey!" Jonathan called after him. "I want an answer please!"

"And he's *answered* it!" Bonnie replied as she placed a round black tray of drinks on the counter. "Now why don't you relax and just *enjoy* yourselves. Here, these *drinks* are on me".

Jonathan looked at her sternly, "You *shouldn't* be serving us alcohol", he said. "This is an underage club!"

Bonnie smiled at him. "I know. It's *not* alcohol. It's a *special* drink I made…for *you* boys. Now drink up!"

Jonathan looked at her suspiciously and then at the drinks. There were three glass bottles on the tray that contained a pink and orange coloured liquid. They were making a fizzing sound as bubbles popped out the top.

"They don't look like any *drinks* I've ever seen!" he exclaimed. "Should they be *bubbling* like that!?"

Before Bonnie could answer Danny came across and grabbed two of the drinks and handed one to Drew.

"Well…don't ya' *trust* me angel?" Bonnie asked smiling at Jonathan. He looked at the others who were waiting for him to come back and join them. There was a part of him that could sense that something wasn't right, but he took the last bottle and rejoined his friends on the dance floor. He didn't see Bonnie grin to herself as they all raised their bottles and took a swig of the mystery liquid.

They felt a tingling sensation sweep through their bodies as they put down the bottles, they stopped and stared off into space, as if in a trance and their eyes slowly began to turn the colour of the liquid.

"LET'S PARTY!!!" Danny suddenly yelled out as he raised his bottle in the air. The others looked at him and then laughed. They couldn't stop themselves. It was like they had forgotten about all their worries and began to enjoy themselves, just like Bonnie had told them to.

Chapter Three
The Big Secret

THE BOYS WERE still laughing when they left the nightclub at a later time of 11:15 and walked down the quiet street as they cast shadows on the wall.

Suddenly Jonathan spoke, "Hey did you guys feel a little *strange* when you drank that drink?" he asked turning to look at them. He had come back to his senses.

Danny smiled at him, "I felt great! *I feel* great dude! It was the *best* drink I ever tasted!"

"No. That was *no* drink", Jonathan told him as he tried to undo his green tie that had somehow gotten around his head. "It didn't *taste* right!"

"Stop dissin' the drink would ya'!" James suddenly piped up from behind.

Jonathan turned round and stopped. "Do you *honestly* think I would put this tie around my head if I was *aware* of it!?" He held up his tie and pointed to his head as he tried to get the others to realise that something had happened to them.

Suddenly a frown formed across Danny's face as he remembered. "He *does* have a point", he said looking at the floor. "Come to think of it I *did* feel a little odd".

"You *are* odd!"

"James!" Jonathan said turning around and frowning at James.

Danny looked worryingly at Jonathan, "Do ya' think she *drugged* us Jonathan!?" he asked.

Drew had also come back to his senses and looked at Jonathan. He noticed that his tracksuit top had become secured tightly around his waist. He untied it as he listened to Jonathan who was annoyed and saying that he wanted to go back and get some answers.

"Chill out!" James said aggressively.

"He's right", Danny told him, "it's late, we'll go back tomorrow". He then turned to look at James, "So James, how was your birthday?"

James closed his eyes, "Oh ya' know, great!" he said sarcastically. "Car rally, free food, underage film, being drugged…and finding out that one of my best *friends* wants to see me *die!*" He opened his eyes and pointed angrily at Drew as the other two gasped and stared at him.

"Oh *come on!*" Jonathan snapped as Drew began to cry again. "You need to *snap* out of it James!"

Danny quickly came in-between James and Drew and placed his arms around their necks as he brought them together. He smiled at James, "Yeah c'mon dude, we're all *friends* here aren't we!? We won't let nothing happen to ya'!"

"Not that *anything* *is* gonna happen!" Jonathan said glaring at James. "The sooner you *realise* that the better!"

"Yeah, us four, we're a *team*, we've got to *stick* together!" Danny said looking at both James and Drew. He slowly removed his arms and placed his hand palm down into the circle. "What do ya' say, all for one…"

The other three looked down at his hand and then Drew placed his on top, "and one…" he said quietly.

"For…" Jonathan continued as he placed his hand on top of Drew's. "James?" Danny asked smiling at him.

James looked down at their hands and frowned, then he gave out a deep sigh and placed his hand on top. "All!" he finished.

Suddenly Jonathan pulled his hand away and gasped as he stared at James open-mouthed. The others looked at him curiously.

"What!?" James asked turning towards him and looking annoyed.

"Nothing!" Jonathan quickly said. "It's just w…well…" He didn't want to cause another argument so tried to think up something to say and was luckily distracted by his watch.

"Oh my God! Look at the *time!*" he exclaimed. "We've got to get *back*!" He looked up and saw that the others were already running towards the bridge.

"LAST ONE BACK GETS A WET WAKE UP CALL TOMORROW MORNING!" he heard Danny scream.

"DANNY I THOUGHT WE SAID *NO MORE* PRANKS!" Jonathan shouted back and they all raced back home as the full moon shone in the night sky.

"Hello? Mr and Mrs Darson? We're back", Jonathan called as they walked through the door and into the hallway.

"Why is it so dark in here?" Danny wondered out loud as they all peered around in the darkness.

"We're up here boys", they heard Mrs Darson's voice call out from upstairs.

They crept up the stairs led by Jonathan and came across some wooden steps on the landing, which lead up to the attic.

"What's going on?" Danny asked. "Why are they *up* there?"

"Could you guys come up here please?" they heard Mrs Darson say.

They looked at each other, wondering what was going on and Danny remembered that she had mentioned a surprise for all of them and thought that this was maybe it.

Jonathan climbed the steps and stared into the attic as he reached the top.

Candlelight had lit up his face and he looked confused by what he saw.

"What's going on up there Jonny boy?" Danny called up to him.

"You guys need to come up here", Jonathan replied.

As the other three reached the top they too all stared at
what they saw for in the room stood all their parents who
were dressed in strange clothing. James's parents and
Drew's father were wearing the same outfit. He looked just
like his son with his brown floppy hair but he wore glasses.
They wore a black short sleeved hooded top, which was
covered in tiny silver stars and matching trousers. They had
a purple band tied around their waists, silver cuffs around
their wrists and a purple headpiece with a silver star in the
centre on their foreheads.

Danny's mother was dressed head to toe in a two-tone
blue cat suit which complimented her long curly ginger
hair. She had blue markings on her face and was holding
her husband's hand. He had short shaven brown hair and
was dressed differently in a long green robe with a black
cape covered in multi-coloured stars. He also had a silver
studded earring in his left ear.

Jonathan's father had shoulder length blond hair which
flicked out at the ends. He wore similar clothing only his
robe was purple and Jonathan's mother was dressed in a
long white flowing dress with a gold band around her waist
and also on her head. She was beautiful and had blue sparkling eyes and shoulder length blonde hair, lighter than her
husbands. She held his hand as she smiled at her son.

Jonathan looked back and then at the contents of the
room. It was small and had wooden floorboards and brown
walls with a small wooden door facing them.

There was a little black shelf in one of the corners,
which was filled with glass bottles of all shapes and sizes

that contained a range of multi-coloured liquids. There were some other strange objects on there too.

Opposite that in another corner was a tall black and gold mirror which Danny was standing next to and then in the other corner was a small round wooden table which had black and gold ancient looking chairs around it and candles on top that lit up the whole room. Around the table stood Jonathan's parents and Drew's father.

Jonathan turned to look at his parents again, "Mother? Father? What are *you* doing here? What's going on?"

"Don't ya' think I'm a bit too *old* for fancy dress parties!?" James said as he closed his eyes.

"This *isn't* a fancy dress party James", his mother replied. "You boys are old enough now to know the *truth!*"

"The *truth*?" Danny looked at them, was this what Matt was talking about earlier?

"Yes. You see…well…there's no easy way to tell you this…" Mrs Darson stuttered as tears began to form in her eyes, "…but…well…you're not…you're not…well…"

Mr Darson put his arm around his wife and tried to comfort her, "What she is *trying* to say is that none of you are *human!*" They stared at him in shock. *"What!?"*

"Excuse me!?"

"What!? But we *act* like humans, *talk* like humans, *look* like humans", Danny said. "How can…"

"But you *are* different", Mr Darson interrupted, "you're all *magical beings!*"

"Oh great!" James said sarcastically. "So we're freaks!"

His father was annoyed at him, "No. Not freaks. *Magical beings*".

"Which is another way of *saying freaks*!"

"You're not a freak!" Mr Darson said angrily and glared at his son. "You're a *witch* James!"

"Jonathan son", Mr Jones said as he looked at his son, "you are half *wizard* and half *angel*!"

"Danny, you're half *wizard* and half *metamorph*!" Mr Murray told him as Danny gave a quick smile.

"Andrew", Mr Fletcher began, "you are half *witch* and…" he paused, "half *seer*".

Jonathan and Danny stared open mouthed at their parents as they tried to take this in but James just frowned at this as Drew looked down at the floor, teardrops rolling down his cheeks.

Suddenly Mr Murray spoke and pointed towards the small wooden door, "At Midnight you boys will pass through, into the vortex and attend *The Academy of Merlin*", he said.

"This is some twisted joke right", James said shaking his head and looking at his parents repulsively. "Magic *isn't* real!" He had had enough and headed back towards the opening of the trapdoor.

The others watched him and gasped as they turned to see silver lightning shooting from Mr Darson's hands and over the trapdoor sealing it shut. James stopped. He was in shock. He was trapped.

"You're not going anywhere James", he heard his father say. "None of you are, except through *here*!"

James slowly turned around and the other three watched with baited breath as the small wooden door began to glow and then slowly opened revealing a big mass of blue and purple swirls which were spinning faster and faster like a tornado.

"What is that!?" asked Jonathan as he stared at it, like he was in a trance.

"That's the vortex to the *other* world which you now must enter", Mr Murray told them. The boys stared into the vortex; it had a hypnotic effect on them as they wondered what the *other* world was and what was on the other side.

Suddenly they were distracted by the sound of a crow in the night sky and they pulled their eyes away from the vortex.

The crow cast a shadow across the full moon and landed on a branch outside the attic window. No one noticed as it peered in with an evil glint in its red eyes.

"I think they're telling the truth James", Jonathan said, "I mean it would *explain* the red sparks I saw coming from your hand!"

Everyone gasped and stared in horror at James. He turned towards Jonathan, "what are you talking about!?" he asked angrily and looked slightly confused.

Jonathan explained. "When you put your hand on mine I saw *red sparks*. It made me tingle!" he told him.

Everyone looked at James and then Mr Jones spoke, "Are you *sure* that's what you saw son?" he asked. He looked concerned.

"Yes Father".

"Then we must do what we must do!" Mr Jones said as both he and Mr Murray raised their hands as balls of light filled in their palms, magic glowing around their fingers. They turned towards James, anger filled their faces and were about to aim when Mrs Darson cried out at the shock of what they were about to do. Tears filled her eyes; she couldn't allow this to happen.

"Joseph! You *can't*!" Jonathan's mother glared at her husband.

"She's right", Mrs Murray agreed, *"you mustn't.* Remember it's about *all* of them!"

Mr Jones looked at Mr Murray and slowly they put down their hands as the balls of light disappeared. Joseph looked at his wife and sighed. "You're right dear, I'm sorry".

"The time has come to say goodbye", she said softly as she walked over to Jonathan who was still a bit in shock.

"Goodbye Jonathan", she whispered in his ear as she hugged him tightly, "stay *safe*. I love you".

"Goodbye son", his father said as he placed his hand on Jonathan's shoulder.

"Good…goodbye. I love you too", Jonathan said as he wondered what was going to happen to them.

"Goodbye son", Mr Murray smiled as both he and his wife flung their arms around Danny. "It's time to grow up now".

"Yeah", Danny whispered.

"I love you Danny!" his mother cried as she squeezed him.

"Don't cry Andrew", Mr Fletcher said as Drew hugged onto him not wanting to let go. They were both crying. "It's gonna be ok", his father tried to reassure him. "You stick with your friends and take care. I love you son".

"James…" Mrs Darson looked at her son as both she and her husband walked over to him.

"Stay away from me *you freaks*!" James spat as he held up his hands for them to back off.

"James!" His father scolded as Mrs Darson began crying into his arms, "You must go through, you *must*!"

James's eyes narrowed. "Oh I'll go through", he said with hatred, "but when I get back, if we *are* coming back, then I am so *outta here*!"

"You *will* come back, you *all* will", Mrs Jones told them, but she looked worried. "Now you must go before it's too late!"

The boys looked at each other and then at their parents. Jonathan took a deep breath and walked towards the vortex as the others watched. "Goodbye then", he said as he turned and waved.

"This isn't goodbye; *it's a new beginning*!" His mother smiled as she waved back.

Danny, Drew and James watched open-mouthed as Jonathan walked into the vortex and disappeared.

Danny walked up next; he was actually excited and couldn't wait to begin this new adventure. He didn't hesitate as he waved goodbye to his parents and walked straight in.

Drew very slowly and still crying walked up to the door and stopped. He looked down at the floor as his father encouraged him to go through.

Suddenly Drew gasped and horror struck his face as Danny's arm reached out of the vortex and grabbed Drew's pulling him in.

"James...", his father said tensely looking at his son.

James looked at them all resentfully, he didn't want any of this, he didn't want to go through but he did want to escape these "freaks" that were surrounding him. He glared at his parents one last time and disappeared into the vortex.

Suddenly the crow that had been watching all this through the window flew into the attic. The adults gasped as they stared at the bird as it flew past them and followed James through the vortex.

Mr Jones turned towards James's parents, "Harry, Rachel, did you *know*?" he asked.

"I assure you we had no idea!" Mr Darson told him.

"Then there is a *possibility* that they may choose the *wrong* path!" Mr Jones announced as he creased his forehead.

"No!" cried out Mrs Darson. "He won't *be* like that!"

Mr Jones looked at her, "We have no idea *what* they'll be like or whether they'll come back at *all*!" He was worried, "but if they do take the *wrong* path..." he said as he turned towards the vortex, "...then we have no choice..." he took a deep breath, "but to *kill* them all!"

They all stared at him in horror knowing that what he had just said was true, they turned towards the vortex praying that they would never have to do the unthinkable and that their children would be safe and be the same when they returned. They felt sick as they watched the vortex slowly disappear.

Chapter Four
Which Way?

"WHERE ARE WE?" Jonathan wondered as he looked at the others. They all looked around at the big, tall, dark trees that were surrounding them. The full moon shone eerily above them. It was very dark and very quiet. The only sound they could hear was their heartbeats. They peered around nervously into the darkness through the trees wondering if they were alone and if they were safe.

"GET DOWN!" they suddenly heard Jonathan shout out as he turned around and saw a big, black shadow coming towards them. They all ducked as a big, black bird flew over their heads and into the trees.

"Well this *sucks*!" James said angrily.

"I *thought* they said we were going to The Academy of Merlin!?" Danny said as he looked at Jonathan.

Jonathan looked around. "Follow me", he said as he walked towards the trees. Danny and Drew looked at each other and followed as James stood there frowning.

"I'm not going *anywhere!*" he called after them.

Jonathan stopped and looked back at him, "Do you want to stay here on your own in some spooky wood, or do you want to *try* and find a way out!?" He asked as he glared at James. He had had enough of James's moody behaviour.

James narrowed his eyes at him, sighed and then reluctantly followed. He wasn't happy about any of this.

They had only walked a little way when Jonathan stopped suddenly. "What's up dude?" Danny asked as he peered over his shoulder trying to see through the darkness.

"There's something up ahead", Jonathan whispered as he caught sight of a bright light in the distance.

"What is it?"

"I don't know", Jonathan told him, "let's just stay together and go find out". He went ahead as Danny stared after him, his heartbeat was racing but he admired Jonathan for being brave and so followed nervously with Drew and James behind.

As they neared the light they could just about make out the outline of a small, wooden shelter and there was something in it.

"It's alright", Jonathan said to the others as he got closer, he could now see that there were four metal pegs along the top and hanging from them were four black fleece jackets. He looked around curiously and then put one on, as did Danny and Drew who were thankful as it was very cold and they weren't wearing many layers.

"I'm not putting on some *jacket*!" James hissed as he looked away.

"Do you want to get *pneumonia*!?" Jonathan asked him angrily.

James huffed. Jonathan was right, if he didn't wear it he would *freeze* to death, so he seized the jacket off the peg and put it on.

They all stopped there for a moment, peering into the trees, waiting for something to happen, but nothing did.

"*Someone* was expecting us", Jonathan whispered to the others; they were all huddled together.

"So what now?" Danny asked him.

"We keep going; we've got to get out of here!" Jonathan told them as he walked on ahead.

"We're right behind ya' Jonny Boy!" Danny replied as he and the other two followed. Jonathan kept his eyes looking ahead in the distance and was highly alert as Danny and Drew nervously watched the trees as they went by and James glared at Jonathan from behind and muttered to himself under his breath.

Jonathan stopped as he came onto a dull yellow stone footpath. "What now?" Danny asked looking at it curiously.

"We follow it", Jonathan answered as he led the way.

They had been walking for about an hour or so it seemed when Danny suddenly froze.

Jonathan turned around as the others stared at him, "What is it?" Jonathan asked.

"I think I saw *something*!" Danny said, his voice shaking.

"Where?"

"Over *there*!" Danny announced pointing towards the big trees on his left. The others slowly turned their heads towards the trees afraid of what Danny had seen as he kept his eyes on Jonathan. He was shaking.

"There's nothing there", Jonathan told him shaking his head as he turned back to look at Danny. "It's just your imagination".

"But I thought I saw…"

"What? What did you think you saw?" Jonathan asked.

"There *was* something there!" Danny whispered, looking concerned. "I think we're *being followed*!"

Suddenly Drew started to shake as his heartbeat increased and tears filled up in his eyes. He was crying again.

"Oh no! Now look what you've gone and done!" Jonathan scolded. "You're scaring him!"

He walked over towards Drew and put his arm around him.

"It's alright", he smiled as he tried to comfort his friend. "Danny has just been watching too many episodes of *Paranormal Patrol* that's all!" He looked up at Danny, the corner of Danny's mouth twitched and then he nodded.

"Yeah", he agreed, "I've just been letting my imagination get the better of me. I'm sorry I didn't mean to scare ya'!"

He walked over and was about to hug Drew when something caught his eye. "Oh my God! *Look*!" he gasped as he stared at the trees.

The others were startled but this time they saw what Danny had seen. Looking back at them, not too far away, from the centre of the trees was a pair of angry looking red glowing eyes!

"F…!" James was about to swear.

"RUN!" Jonathan yelled!

They all ran as fast and as far as they could, wondering whether that thing, whatever it was, was following them. They shuddered at the thought of what was lurking in this dark, scary wood. They just wanted to get out.

"SEE! I TOLD YOU!", Jonathan heard Danny yell, he also heard Drew crying again.

Jonathan didn't look back, none of them did, they just kept running and running and didn't stop even when their sides began to ache. They just had to get safe.

Suddenly they came to an opening. There were two paths leading off in opposite directions and two signposts pointing in the directions of the paths. There was writing on both.

Jonathan stopped then to read them.

"Don't…stop… Jon…" Danny panted as he entered the clearing, "choose… a path!"

Jonathan turned around as James also came into view shortly followed by Drew who was in a right state.

"I think it's ok", Jonathan told them as he cautiously peered through the trees. "I don't think it followed us".

"How can…you be… sure?" Danny coughed looking at him as he held his hands on his sides trying to get his breath back.

"I am sure", Jonathan stated as he turned to look at the signposts.

Danny and James walked over to him as Drew collapsed by their feet. He was exhausted and coughing heavily.

Danny sat down beside him and tried to calm him down. "So *which way* Jonathan?" he asked.

"I don't know", Jonathan replied still looking at the signs. The one on the left read:

HERE'S A CHOICE YOU MUST MAKE,

DECIDE WHICH PATH, YOU ARE TO TAKE.

MANY BEFORE YOU HAVE CHOSEN THE RIGHT WAY,

BUT WE NEED YOU THROUGH OUR DOORS TODAY.

FOR SOME WILL SEE, AND I HOPE YOU DO TOO

THAT IT IS THE WRONG WAY FOR YOU!

THINK CAREFULLY AT WHAT YOU MUST DO!

The one on the right was shorter and more to the point, it read:

EVIL RISES!

MAKE THE RIGHT CHOICE!

"Well it's *obvious* isn't it!?" James said as he read the signs, "we go *right*!" He headed off towards the right path.

"Wait!" Jonathan called. "I'm not so sure".

"Look at the sign, it says make the *right* choice!" James was starting to get angry again.

All of a sudden they jumped at a sound coming from high above them. They looked up and saw that a big, black crow had been watching them and was perched on a large branch on a tree from the right hand path. They watched as it crowed loudly and then flew off a little way towards the right. It then sat on another branch in the next tree and turned to look at them, it then flew off and into another tree crowing each time as it looked at the four boys.

"We go right!" James said and he continued towards the path.

"James *wait*!" Jonathan urged as he turned to read the signs again, trying to decide which path to take.

"It's a *sign*!" James announced pointing to the bird. "It clearly wants us to *follow* it!"

"We go *left*!" Jonathan suddenly said.

Danny and Drew looked at him and then at James and then they got up and headed towards Jonathan.

James looked annoyed. "What makes you so sure it's that way!?" he demanded as he stopped and stared at them.

"Take a look", Jonathan said, pointing to the left-hand signpost. "I worked it out".

James slowly walked back and looked at the words. He couldn't see anything. "Well?" he asked.

Jonathan pointed it out. "It says *'many before you have chosen the right way...'*"

"Yeah, so we go *that* way!" James interrupted.

Jonathan frowned at him, "It says that it is the *wrong* way!"

James shook his head as he stared at the sixth line of the verse and then pointed to the right hand sign. "This one says *'make the right choice!'*"

"It also says *'Evil rises!'*" Jonathan told him pointing to the words above. "We're going *left* ". He turned and headed towards the left-hand path as Danny and Drew followed him.

"Hold on!" James snapped. "Why should we follow *you!?* You're not our leader!"

Danny and Drew looked at Jonathan who sighed. "No, but I am the *eldest*".

"So *what!?*" James said angrily. "Doesn't mean we have to do what you *say* all the time!"

Jonathan huffed; he was really starting to get irritated by James. "We're going *this* way, and if you want to go the other way, then fine! Come on guys!"

Danny followed him up the path but stopped and looked at James. "Come on dude, we've gotta stick together remember?!" he said smiling at him. "You know he's right. He's *always* right!" He rolled his eyes.

"Well you're *wrong!*" James replied, " 'cos he wasn't right about *one* thing!"

"And what's *that*?" Jonathan called back as he heard the conversation.

"Him!" James said angrily pointing at Drew. *"You* said that they were just *stupid dreams*, that *nothing* was gonna happen. Well guess what, you were *wrong!*"

"Nothing *is* going to happen!" Jonathan snapped back.

"Newsflash!" James spat. "He's a damn *Seer*!"

Jonathan looked at Drew who was starting to cry again. He was right. "I didn't know that then", he said softly. He was calmer now.

"Well you do *now*!" James hissed. "And I'm gonna *die*!"

"You're not going to die James", Jonathan said as he walked back. "We're not gonna let it".

"You can't stop it", James said shaking his head. "It's gonna happen!"

"Well...we'll try and prevent it", Jonathan told him. "We're going to stick *together* and we're going to *protect* you".

James sighed. "You can't".

"Yes we can!" Jonathan assured him. "We've just got to keep you away from fire that's all!"

James looked at him and wondered why Jonathan would still want to be friends with him after his behaviour.

"I'm sorry", he apologised, "you're right, we'll go your way". He flashed Jonathan a quick smile and then headed towards the left-hand path and apologised to Drew as he walked past.

Jonathan and Danny smiled at each other but both were thinking about how on earth they were going to stop Drew's vision from coming true.

They walked towards the path and followed James who led the way, making sure that Drew was alright, they didn't want him feeling any guilt about his premonitions.

They didn't hear the crow take off from the tree branch or see as a red glow suddenly appeared around its feathers and it changed shape taking on the form of a small fly. It followed them up the path and then it very carefully placed itself on Danny's back.

Chapter Five

Reception

THEY FOLLOWED THE path as it wound through more trees and then went up a hill. "Look", James said suddenly as he pointed to a small building that was sat at the top.

The others looked. It was a small stone brown building which had a chimney on top and smoke was coming out.

"Come on then", Jonathan suggested as he walked past the others and led the way again up the hill.

"Is that the Academy?" Danny wondered as he caught up with Jonathan.

"I don't know", Jonathan replied. He kept his eyes on the building, as did the others looking at it curiously as they wondered what was inside. One thing they knew for sure was that it had a fire and so was going to be warmer than outside in the wood.

As they neared the top they noticed that a thick fog had come out of nowhere and was now surrounding the boys. They couldn't see the trees around them anymore, just the fog which was growing thicker by the minute.

"Is this such a good idea?" Danny asked as he stared at the fog around them.

"Well I'm not going *back*", Jonathan answered as he walked up to the door. The others peered over his shoulder at the black iron door. There was no handle or bell just two little oval shapes at the top, an eyes width apart.

"Now what?" Danny shrugged as he looked at Jonathan. "How do we get *in*?"

Jonathan looked carefully at the door. "I'll just knock", he concluded. He raised his hand and knocked three times on the door.

They all jumped back in shock as the oval shapes at the top opened to reveal a pair of blue eyes staring back at them.

Drew cowered behind Danny as they all froze staring at the eyes. They were all terrified as the eyes closed and the door slowly creaked open.

"I'm *scared*!" Drew whispered, his voice shaking.

"You're not the only one!" Danny confessed.

Jonathan took a deep breath and then walked up to the door cautiously, his heart racing as he tried to peer inside.

"You're not going *in*!?" James called after him.

"Well I'm not staying out *here*!" Jonathan replied and he took another deep breath and walked through the door.

The other three looked at each other and then at the fog that had now covered the path, it was closing in around them.

"Let's go", Danny said as he walked up to the door, "it's got to be *safer* than out here!"

Drew nodded and kept close to Danny as they neared the door whilst James looked on nervously.

"But there's fire in there!" he said suddenly.

Danny turned around, "Yeah, so it's gonna be *warm*", he said smiling.

"But...that's *how* it happens", James said, there was fear in his voice, "it's how I...*die!*"

"We're not gonna let you die dude", Danny assured him. "Come on".

James looked at him, took a deep breath and followed Danny and Drew into the building. It was dark inside and the only light was coming from five candles along both the left and right hand stone walls. They could see that there were white tiles on the floor.

They all jumped at the sound of the door slamming behind them and the flames of the candles blew out. They were in complete darkness.

"Well there's no turning back *now!*" Jonathan whispered as the other three huddled around him nervously.

"This is *it*", James gulped. "This is his stupid vision. I'm gonna *die!*"

"You're *not* going to die!" Jonathan told him. "It was a vision in the *future*, not now!"

"But I'm still gonna die *eventually*!"

"Well we *all* are; that's life!"

Suddenly they stared ahead as they saw another door open up slightly in front of them revealing light and a gentle, female voice spoke to them. "Well aren't you going to come through?" it said. "We've been expecting you".

The four boys looked at each other and then looked at the door. "Stay close", Jonathan told them as he led the way towards the door, their heartbeats were starting to get louder as Jonathan pushed open the black, iron door and very cautiously peered inside the room. He didn't see anyone as he looked at the room. It was small and seemed cosy due to the large flames that were coming out of a large fireplace in the far end, left hand corner. He felt the warmth as he and the others entered the room.

They stood on a light purple coloured carpet as they looked around. The walls were a pale yellow and there was a black velvet sofa against the right hand wall and a wooden varnished round table next to it the same length as the sofa. They saw another black, iron door ahead of them, the fire was next to it and there were another two doors on the left-hand wall and in front of one of them was a large desk full of paperwork stacked up in neat piles on one of the corners. Next to that was a small black pencil pot, full of pens and a computer on the other side of the desk. There was a black velvet swivel chair at the desk and they were startled as they watched it spin around and saw a young woman sitting in it.

She smiled at them as Jonathan, Danny and Drew looked at her and James kept glancing across at the fire. His heartbeat racing.

She was older than the boys, seemed about in her twenties Jonathan thought as he eyed her suspiciously. She had short-cropped dark purple hair, had blue sparkling eyes which were covered by some gold pointy spectacles and wore pale pink make-up.

She was dressed in a white shirt with an indigo coloured blazer and had a red tie around her neck.

"Hello", she said, her voice was gentle, "don't be afraid, you're safe now". She got up and held out her hand, "I'm Kirsty. Who are you four?"

Jonathan told her who they all were as they all shook her hand wondering if she was friend or foe.

"Excuse me", Jonathan said after they had all been introduced, "is this the Academy?"

Kirsty smiled, "No, this is reception", she said as she opened a small wooden cupboard next to the desk and brought out four plates and placed them on a white varnished work unit which the boys hadn't noticed before. There was also a white kettle in the corner, which she switched on.

"Did we choose the *right* path?" Jonathan asked as he watched her take four black mugs from the cupboard and place them onto the unit next to the plates.

"I can't tell you that", she replied, her back was turned as she put two spoonfuls of drinking chocolate powder into each mug. "If I told you that you were about to attend The Dark Academy then you would try and escape, and if you *wanted* to attend The Dark Academy and found out you were to attend The Academy of Merlin you would also try to escape".

"We *want* to attend The Academy of Merlin", Jonathan told her, as he looked at the other three who all nodded. "By the way, what *is* The Dark Academy?"

"The Dark Academy is similar to The Academy of Merlin, only it's for *evil*", Kirsty told them.

"We don't *want* to be evil", Jonathan looked at her with a worried look on his face.

"I'm sorry", Kirsty replied as she added some milk to the mugs. "I'm sorry, but I'm not allowed to say. You'll find out when you get there".

"And *when* will we be there?" James asked, still keeping his eyes on the fire.

"Tomorrow morning", Kirsty smiled, "but first you must fill out a form. And you must all be starving so here", she turned around and handed them each a plate. There were seven chocolate chip cookies on each.

"Thank you", Jonathan smiled as he took his plate.

Danny and Drew were also grateful but James took his without a word and just looked at Kirsty and the food suspiciously.

"You can sit over there", Kirsty told them and pointed to the black sofa.

The boys took their plates and walked over to the sofa where they placed them down on the table and looked at each other.

"Do you think they're *ok* to eat?" Danny asked Jonathan curiously as they all looked at the biscuits but before Jonathan could answer Kirsty came over and placed two mugs down on the table which were now full of steaming hot chocolate and had whipped cream and marshmallows on top.

"Drink up!" Kirsty smiled at them.

"This *has* to be the right path", Danny concluded as he breathed in the luxurious chocolaty aroma. "Would evil do *this* for us!?"

James was about to say something but stopped as Kirsty came back with the other two mugs and looked at them all. "Is something *wrong*?" she asked.

"No! Not at all!" Jonathan said quickly as the others shook their heads.

"Good", she smiled, "I'll get the paperwork. Enjoy your supper".

They watched quietly as she went over to the desk and took four pieces of paper from one of the piles and also four black pens from a pot. She returned and handed them each a sheet. "Please fill this in", she said to them. "When you're finished and finished your meal please come over to the desk and then you can do the next step before I send you on your way".

They smiled and nodded obediently and took a seat on the sofa as she walked away and sat opposite them at her desk and began typing on the computer.

"Evil *wouldn't* do this for us", Danny whispered as he glanced up at Kirsty, "we've got hot chocolate *with* marshmallows, *marshmallows!*"

"Has it ever occurred to you that this could be all part of her plan to get us to *trust* her!" James frowned as he whispered back. He was sitting the furthest away from the fire next to Danny.

"She seems nice enough", Jonathan said glancing up at her, "and this *feels* right".

"Alright then", James said looking past Danny and Drew, "*eat* a cookie, *drink* your drink".

Jonathan looked at him and then looked down at his plate and also his drink. It did smell delicious but he was aware that he had drunk something before that turned out to be something it wasn't. He very cautiously took a biscuit from his plate as the others watched open mouthed. Kirsty looked up as the cookie touched his lips.

Jonathan slowly opened his mouth and took a tiny bite of the cookie. He chewed as his heartbeat increased. What was going to happen to him?

Nothing did happen.

"Well", Danny asked, "how you feeling?"

"Normal", replied Jonathan as he took another bite. "Try them they're *delicious!*"

"You've only eaten *one*", James stated.

"Yeah, and it's fine!" Jonathan told him.

"Doesn't mean that the *others* are!"

Jonathan stared at him. "Eat them *all!*"

"James, why do you always have to have a *suspicious* mind!?"

Danny and Drew looked at Jonathan and then at the remaining cookies on his plate. He could see that they were thinking the same. "Fine!" he huffed and they watched as Jonathan munched on his cookies until they had all gone.

"There!" he said after he had swallowed the last biscuit. *"I'm fine!* Now *eat* them!"

The other three reached for their plates and took small bites of the cookies as Kirsty looked down and grinned to herself.

"Alright, drink the *drink* then!" James said as he munched on his cookie. They really were as good as Jonathan had said.

"You drink it!" Jonathan suggested, looking at him angrily.

"No way!" James replied.

"I tested the cookies!"

"And now *you* can test the drink!"

"Look, I'm *not* a guinea pig!" Jonathan snapped back.

"I'll drink it!" Danny said sensing the tension. He reached out and took his mug off the table and brought it towards his lips as the others looked on.

The heat of the mug felt good around his hands and the smell made his mouth water. He took a sip.

Kirsty looked up again and Drew giggled when Danny removed his cup to reveal a creamy moustache.

"What!?" he asked looking at them as they tried not to laugh.

"You've got something there", Jonathan told him touching his own top lip. Danny wiped away the cream with the back of his arm.

"It's fine", he told them. "You should taste it, it's *gorgeous*!"

The other three smiled and they too took sips of their drinks.

"You really shouldn't worry so much", Kirsty suddenly spoke. "I told you, you're *safe* here".

Jonathan smiled at her. "Yeah, sorry", he nodded. "Can't be too careful y'know".

She smiled and then returned to her work as Jonathan looked at his form. The others did the same.

"We gonna fill these out then?" Danny asked him.

"Of course".

"Should we *lie*!" James grinned glancing up at Kirsty.

"No James, we shouldn't!" Jonathan told him, "now let's just get these done shall we", he looked down at his form and started filling it out. The others watched him and then did the same.

"Are we really gonna tell them where we *live*!?" James asked as he read one of his questions.

"Yes". Jonathan hissed.

"What if we're going to *The Dark Academy*!" James said worryingly, "I don't want evil *knowing* where I live!"

"We're not *going* to The Dark Academy!" Jonathan said looking up.

"How can you be so *sure*?" James wondered as he frowned at Jonathan.

"It just *feels* right".

James stared at Jonathan as he continued to fill in his form.

Danny looked at James. "Look dude, if he's wrong you can hit him!"

"Hey!" Jonathan heard him and looked up annoyed at Danny.

"What!?" Danny shrugged. *"If* you're right then you have nothing to worry about! It can be James's way of saying I *told you so*!" He gave Jonathan a quick grin and closed his eyes and then quickly put his head down and got back to filling in his form.

Chapter Six
No Way Out

JONATHAN STARED AT him, sighed and shook his head as he filled in the last question on the form.

"I'm finished", he announced as he got up and walked over to the desk. The others watched as Kirsty looked up and took the form off him.

"Now please go through this door", she said smiling and pointed to the black iron door that was a little way from behind her desk on the left-hand wall. "Just fill out the questions *truthfully*, as your answers will determine *where* to put you".

"What do you mean?" Jonathan asked her curiously, "What *Academy* I'm going to?"

"No", Kirsty smiled shaking her head, "you'll go to the Academy that is on *this* path. This will decide your group".

"My *group*?" Jonathan looked confused.

"Please, just go through", Kirsty urged as she waved her hand at the door.

Danny, Drew and James watched Jonathan walk over to the door. He turned around to look at them and then slowly opened the door as he wondered what was in *this* room.

"Remember, answer *truthfully*", Kirsty reminded him as he entered the room. It was a small, square room, which had a dark red carpet and white walls. There was nothing in it except for a desk at the far end on which sat a small computer.

Jonathan walked over to it and sat in the black, velvet swivel chair, which was next to it and looked as a question suddenly appeared on the screen. He was about to start typing in his answer when he heard the door shut behind him.

In the other room James got up alarmed as he stared at Kirsty. "*Why* did you shut him in there!?" he demanded.

Kirsty looked at him and smiled. "You really need to calm down James", she said. "He's just filling out some more questions and you three mustn't see his answers".

"Why not?" James asked.

"Because we want to put you in the *right* group, that's best suited to *you*", she told them. "We don't want you copying your friends answers so that you're in the *same* group, we want to put you where you *belong*!"

"But we want to be *together*!" Danny too, got up and looked at her worryingly, as did Drew.

"I'm sorry", Kirsty said shaking her head, "you'll just have to hope you all have similar personalities. We need you to answer truthfully to make sure we've put you in the right group. If not, then there could be problems".

"What *kind* of problems?" James wondered as he narrowed his eyes.

Before Kirsty could answer, the door opened and Jonathan walked out. They all looked at him.

"I'm done", he said looking at Kirsty.

"Good. Thank you Jonathan. You are now ready". She took him over to the door that was opposite the entrance, on the far wall. "Go inside and close the door behind you", she told him.

Jonathan looked at her and then at the other three. "I'll wait for my friends", he smiled.

"You must go *now*", Kirsty told him nodding. "Only *one* can go at a time". Jonathan looked at her puzzled. He then turned to the others.

"I'll see you soon", he said and he opened the door and peered inside. The room was completely dark; he couldn't see anything inside. He looked at Kirsty nervously as she urged him to go inside.

"It's ok", she told him. "Remember to close the door behind you".

Jonathan took one last look at his friends before stepping inside. He slowly closed the door behind him and stood in the darkness. He didn't like this one bit and didn't know what to expect. He began to wonder whether this was the right path after all.

Suddenly the room lit up in a blinding white light; Jonathan shielded his eyes with his arm. The light dimmed a bit and Jonathan slowly removed his arm and stared at the range of colours that were now dancing over the walls and creating patterns.

He was startled when a deep male voice spoke out to him. He turned around but no one was there.

"Welcome to the Academy", it said. "You are about to attend a magical place full of mystical creatures and will be your home from now on".

Jonathan was about to ask if it was "The Academy of Merlin" but the voice continued to speak.

"There are four groups at The Academy. Fire, Water, Earth and Air. You will be placed in one of those groups from the answers you have just given and join those in that group".

"What group am..." Jonathan was about to ask which group he was in but the voice interrupted him.

"You will learn how to perfect your magic and gain stars for your group and the group with the most stars at the end of each term will be rewarded", Jonathan listened.

"When you attend this Academy you will need the following: A backpack, a pencil case, notepad, a Timetable, a Rulebook, a Mirror Gem, Library Card and a Key".

Jonathan watched as the objects mentioned appeared suddenly in front of him and began floating around him and then the small, black backpack appeared magically onto his back. He could feel the other objects inside.

"You are about to enter the world of occult, now have a good night's sleep and I'll see you tomorrow", the voice said to him and Jonathan watched in horror as the room disappeared around him and turned into another. This one was different. It was a small stone room with wooden floorboards. There were only four beds in the room, covered in big, white duvets and fluffy pillows. It was dimly lit from the light hanging in the centre of the room.

Jonathan looked at the beds and then at the room. There were no windows and no doors. He was alone.

"Where am I?" he wondered. He put his backpack on one of the beds and then started to feel the walls hoping to find a secret door or any way out.

"Hello?" he called out hoping that someone would hear. No one did.

Jonathan froze as he turned around and saw a bright light suddenly appear in the middle of the room; his heart raced as a dark shadow appeared in the centre of it.

"Jonathan?" Danny said staring at him as he emerged into the room. The light disappeared around him.

Jonathan looked relieved. "Danny", he smiled and took a deep breath. Danny looked around the room, "*where* are we?" he asked.

"I don't know", replied Jonathan as he shook his head.

"What are you doing?" Danny asked him curiously as Jonathan continued to feel the walls.

"Trying to find a way out".

"Well there *has* to be a way out", Danny told him, "we can't just be *stuck* here!" He walked over to the walls and also began searching frantically for a way out.

All of a sudden Danny called out as he noticed a bright white light appearing in the room.

"Er Jon, I don't want to alarm ya' but *something's* happening!"

Jonathan turned around, it was just like before when Danny had appeared, he wasn't so nervous this time, but Danny was and froze as the shape of a human figure emerged in the centre of the light.

"We're *not* alone!" Danny gasped, his heartbeat increased.

"It's ok", Jonathan reassured him, "this is how *you* appeared".

Danny looked at him and then turned to see Drew standing in the middle of the room. He looked worried as he stared at them and then at the room.

"*Where* are we?" he asked nervously.

"*Stuck!*" Danny answered.

"No! We're not stuck!" Jonathan quickly told him. "We just haven't found the way out yet, that's all".

Drew looked at him and then at Danny. He was worried. He didn't like being in a room with no way out.

"Just start feeling over the walls", Jonathan told him.

"What about trap doors?" Danny suggested.

"Good thinking", Jonathan nodded at him. "Check the floor as well and under the beds".

Drew did as he was told as he got down on the wooden floor and looked carefully around for an exit, he wasn't keen on looking under the beds so Danny checked there instead. There was nothing.

"*What* are you all doing?" they heard a familiar voice say.

They jumped and then turned around to see that James had now joined them in the room, his eyebrows raised as he looked at them.

"We're trying to find a way out", Jonathan told him, "but it doesn't look like there is one!" He looked at the other two and shook his head.

"Don't be silly", James frowned, "there *has* to be a way out!"

"We've checked", Jonathan replied.

"Well check again!"

"*You* check!" Jonathan told him angrily as he sat down on one of the beds. It was nice and soft.

Danny and Drew did the same as James looked at them. "So what now Jonathan?" Danny asked.

"I don't know", he replied, his eyes were closed as he sat there thinking. Suddenly he remembered something. He opened his eyes. "The *backpack*!" he said grabbing the bag off the bed; he looked at the emblem on the front. It was gold, a star surrounded by a circle with a triangle in its centre. He hastily opened the zipper. "There might be *something* inside!"

The others watched as he shook out the objects onto the bed. He rummaged through his pencil case and flicked through his notepad, Rulebook, and looked carefully at his Timetable and the small, white, plastic library card which had his name on it in fancy gold lettering. There wasn't anything to help them; even the small gold key was useless as there was no keyhole anywhere in the room.

He sighed. It wasn't looking good.

"What about *that*?" Danny wondered pointing at the Gem that had fallen on the floor.

Jonathan picked it up and looked at it carefully. It was a small, diamond shaped, crystal gem, no bigger than a £2 coin.

The others watched, but nothing happened.

"Maybe we should put them *together*", Danny suggested as he took off his backpack and searched for his Gem, both Drew and James copied him.

They all found their Gems and held them in the palms of their hands. They got up from the beds and huddled together, they then slowly moved the Gems to their fingertips and the Gems touched. They watched and waited with baited breath for something to happen but nothing did.

"Well that's just *great*!" James huffed as he threw his Gem back into his bag, "We're not getting out of here, we're *trapped*!"

Drew's bottom lip started to tremble.

"We're *not* trapped!" Jonathan told James angrily as he noticed that Drew was going to be upset again. "We just don't *know* the way out!"

"*Face* it!" James frowned; "you took us down the *wrong* path!"

"No I *didn't*!" Jonathan was starting to get irritated now and Drew was in tears, he didn't want to go to The

Dark Academy. Danny walked over to him and put his arm around him, trying to comfort him.

"Let's look at the *facts* shall we!?" James; stated, "Our parents send us to some *spooky* wood in the *dark* with something *evil* lurking in it, there's this *scary* looking door with *eyes* in it, we enter *darkened* rooms, and now they've *trapped* us! Would good really want us to *fear* everything!"

"I *don't* want to be evil!" Drew cried out and buried his face in Danny's arms.

Danny stared at James and then at Jonathan. He looked horrified. James was *right*. It had been a terrifying journey.

Jonathan looked at them all and then shook his head. "We're *not* going to be evil", he said but there was doubt in his voice. "This has to be the *right* path!" He sat back down on his bed as he felt the eyes of the other three on him.

"What we gonna do?" Danny asked him as he took a deep breath.

"There's *nothing* we can do", Jonathan whispered, "only sleep". He got up and pulled back the covers on his bed. He took off his white trainers and black fleeced jacket and got inside. It was cosy and warm.

Danny, Drew and James watched him as he lay down and pulled the duvet over his body. "Evil wouldn't give us this *comfort*", he said as he closed his eyes.

The other three looked at each other and then they too kicked off their trainers, took off their jackets and got into the beds.

"But they would *watch* us!" James responded as he looked around the room.

Jonathan opened his eyes. *"What!?"* he moaned.

"It just feels like we're being *watched* that's all!" James told him as he looked carefully around the room. Danny did the same as Drew pulled the covers up to his face, looking terrified.

"We're *not* being watched!" Danny quickly said as he noticed Drew's expression.

"Yes we *are!*"

"Look! Just go to *sleep* James!" Jonathan ordered. He was starting to get annoyed at James again. He knew that Drew would be feeling scared and truth be told he was a bit too. He closed his eyes and prayed that he had taken his friends down the right path.

James huffed and mumbled to himself as he threw the duvet over his body, as Danny looked across at Drew in the next bed. "It's ok", he reassured him, "we're gonna be fine. There's *no one* here but us". He wished him goodnight and pulled the duvet over himself.

Drew sat there for a moment, watching him and then nervously looked around the room. He couldn't see any-thing. He quickly hid himself under his duvet, wrapping it around him like cotton wool. He was shaking. James was right. There *was* something there; he could *feel* it too.

Unbeknown to them, in the top left-hand corner of the room was the fly. It had flown off Danny's back and onto the wall as he had entered the room. It was now watching the boys as they slept, unaware of its presence. It waited. Its red eyes glowed in the darkness.

The boys fell asleep as the building began spinning and floated around in a sea of mystical colours in the night sky. They were heading towards one of the Academy's, but which one were they about to attend?

Chapter Seven
The Academy

"WAKE UP!" JONATHAN told the others as he woke up the next day.

Danny stirred in his bed and slowly sat up. "What?" He yawned as he wiped the sleep from his eyes.

"*Something's* happening", Jonathan told him as he sat staring at the stone wall in front of them.

Danny looked to where Jonathan was staring as James and Drew sat up in their beds. They noticed a bright green laser cutting into the wall from the outside. They watched nervously as the laser went up, and then before it reached the top it turned right.

"It's making a *door*", Jonathan said as the laser went down again.

"Well at least we're getting *out!*" Danny smiled as he nodded at Drew who still looked terrified.

"Yeah, but what's out *there*?" James wondered as he looked at the other three.

"Looks like we're going to find out!" Jonathan answered as the outline of the door in the stone began to tremble.

"You may want to take *cover*!" they heard a male Irish voice call out from behind the door.

They stared open mouthed at the door which was about to fall. They looked at each other and then quickly cowered behind their duvets, shielding their faces as they heard a very loud crash. The door had come down.

They started coughing as dust filled the room and very slowly they all peered over their duvets at the hole in the wall. They couldn't see anything, just a lot of dust which filled the doorway.

"Well, don't you want to come out?" they heard the same voice ask.

The boys looked at each other and then glanced at the doorway. The dust was disappearing now and they could see concrete on the other side, but there was no one there.

Jonathan took a deep breath and got out of his bed as the others watched him put on his trainers and jacket. He also picked up his backpack and put it on.

"You're going *out*!?" Danny asked him.

"Yes", Jonathan nodded; "we're *all* going out, let's all stay *close* ok?"

Once they were ready Danny, Drew and James got behind Jonathan as he led them slowly towards the door, none of them took their eyes off it as their heartbeats increased, fearing for what was out there, in the unknown.

As Jonathan stepped out of the doorway he was greeted by a very handsome young man. He seemed to be about eighteen years of age, slim built, and had short, spiky brown hair and brown eyes. He was dressed in a long-sleeved white shirt and dark blue jeans.

"Hello", he said in his Irish accent, "I'm Ben Meyers, welcome to the *Academy of Merlin!*"

The boys looked relieved, they had chosen the right path after all.

"Hi!" Jonathan smiled at Ben. "Pleased to meet you". He held out his hand and introduced himself and his friends.

"So this is The Academy", Danny said as he looked at the surroundings. They were standing in a huge courtyard which had a stone silver fountain in the centre and silver benches were placed at the sides of the yard next to the huge white walls that surrounded it. It was empty.

"Yep!" Ben said smiling at them. "Come on, I'll show you around".

They followed as he led the way and headed to a big golden gate just right of the fountain.

"How did you get us out of there?" Danny asked curiously as he shoved a thumb over his shoulder indicating back towards the building.

"With this", Ben replied and held up a kind of neon green pen.

"A pen!?" Danny looked disbelieving.

"It's not a pen", Ben told him, "it's a laser wand".

"Cool!" smiled Danny. "Can I have one?"

"No!" Ben grinned, shaking his head and putting the laser wand in his pocket. "It's not mine anyway, it's Master Arthur's".

"Who?" Jonathan asked looking at him.

Ben stopped and turned to look at them all. "Master Arthur is the Head of the Academy", he told them. "You'll meet him after I've given you the tour".

The friends looked at each other.

"Now this is Mystic Meadows", Ben told them as he entered through the gates and raised his arm out behind him at the long emerald coloured grassland behind.

Jonathan, Danny, Drew and James stepped through the gates, taking in the surroundings as Ben led them through the Meadow.

"It's *beautiful* !" Danny gasped as he watched some pretty pink butterflies dance around him.

"It *changes* too", Ben turned to look at them, "the sky, the grass, it's a *magical* place to be!"

"Totally cool!" Danny beamed as he looked up at the sky, it was still the normal colour. *"When* will it change?"

"During the day", Ben smiled as he continued through the Meadow and passed a small river which sparkled a crystal blue as the sunlight bounced off the surface, "but you should see it at night, the sunsets here are *amazing*!"

"Wow!" Danny said excitedly, he was going to love it here. He loved colour.

"Most of the students come here during their free periods, or just to relax", Ben said as they passed a brown haired couple who looked up as they went past. "It can also be very *romantic*". They watched as he picked up a small beautiful pale pink flower and looked at it. He smiled before placing it on to his bright green belt.

"Oh! I haven't asked have I?" he suddenly realised as he turned to look at them. "*What* are you?"

"*What* are we!? Oh, yeah um..." Jonathan suddenly realised what he meant, "well I'm part wizard and part angel".

"Uh-huh, and you?" he asked looking at Danny.

"Half wizard and half something else, what was it? Met? Meta...?" he looked at Jonathan, trying to think what his father had said. It seemed a long time ago now.

"*Metamorph?*" Ben asked raising his eyebrows.

"Yeah *that's* it!" Danny smiled at him; "I'm part Metamorph. *What* is that?"

Ben grinned at him; "You're going to have a lot of *fun* Danny", he said. "You can be *anything* you want to be!"

"Really!?" Danny looked at him in awe.

"Yep!" Ben nodded. "Metamorphs are a kind of *Shapeshifter!*"

"*Awesome!*" Danny grinned. He was definitely going to love it here. "So what about you two?" Ben asked looking at Drew and James.

"I'm half witch and half Seer", Drew told him timidly.

"A *Seer*?" Ben looked at him, "you had any visions?"

Drew looked at Jonathan who cautiously shook his head so that Ben didn't see. "No", Drew answered as he put his head down.

"Liar!" James glared angrily at him.

Ben looked at him and then back at Drew.

"Drew?"

Drew didn't say anything as he stared at the ground.

Ben looked at James who was still glaring at Drew. *"James?"* he asked.

James wasted no time in telling Ben about Drew's vision as Jonathan and Danny stared at him horrified.

"*Why* did you say no?" Ben asked looking at Drew once James had finished telling him. Drew looked like he was about to cry again.

"*I* told him to!" Jonathan admitted.

"Why?"

"I'm sorry", Jonathan said as he hung his head "but we don't know you, and well, I didn't know whether it was normal, should he be having *these* kinds of visions?"

Ben looked at him. "He's a Seer, he's *meant* to have visions", he said.

"Even visions of *death*?" Jonathan asked.

"Seers have visions about *anything* and *everything*", Ben told him and then looked at Drew. "It's ok; it's not wrong".

Drew looked up, he was teary eyed again. He sniffed and then looked away.

"So I *am* gonna die!?" James said fiercely.

"Not necessarily", Ben replied turning to look at him; "you don't know how the vision ends".

"But I get burnt *alive!* How could I possibly *survive* that!?"

"Well, *what* are you James?"

"Witch".

Ben nodded. "Well you *could* survive that I suppose", he said looking up at the sky as he thought about it. He didn't know *how*, but he didn't want to tell them that James *was* going to die. He had to give them some hope.

"So what are *you*?" Jonathan asked Ben as he quickly changed the subject. They all looked at him curiously.

Ben smiled. "I'm a Mer-Boy".

"Yeah right!" James smirked, shaking his head, "where's your *tail?*"

Ben looked at him, still smiling, "It only appears in water", he told him, "come on, let me show you inside the Academy". He turned around and headed back towards the golden gate.

As they left the Meadow, Danny turned round to see that the sky was beginning to change colour, it was turning a warm yellow and the grass was now a light purple.

Cool! he thought to himself and smiled.

"What's that gate?" Jonathan asked Ben when they returned to the courtyard. He pointed to a huge, silver gate on the opposite wall.

"That way leads to Tuskian Town", Ben told them.

"What's Tuskian Town?" Jonathan looked at him curiously.

"It's a place you can go, when you're old enough, just into the Town, shop around, meet people, go for a drink, y'know, like a normal Town, just a little bit more *magical*".

"Can *we* go to the Town?" Danny asked.

"No, you're not *old* enough yet", Ben replied.

"How old do we have to be?"

"Sixteen".

"Are *you* old enough?"

"Yeah, I'm eighteen, in my final year".

"Have you been into town?"

"Yeah, but it's very *dangerous* though".

They looked at him.

"Why?" Jonathan asked.

"Because *everyone* can get to the Town", Ben told them. "It's not just for the students here, but for the students at The Dark Academy too".

"Are they *evil*?" Jonathan stared at him, as did the others.

"Yes, they learn Black Magic, so that's why you need the amulet".

"The *amulet*?" Danny looked puzzled.

"Yes. If you want to go into Town you tell Master Arthur and he'll give you an amulet which will *protect* you against evil".

"Cool!" Danny smiled.

"So that's what it's like on the outside, now let's take you in", Ben said as he turned around and led them up some big white stone steps and into the big white building which Jonathan thought resembled a Museum with its large stone pillars on either side.

As they went through the doors, they entered a huge hallway. The floor was covered in white tiles and the walls and ceiling were black and covered in tiny silver sparkling stars.

"Wow!" Danny looked amazed as he looked up at the ceiling. There were candles above them in a kind of chandelier which was hanging above them.

There was a small gold door on the left hand wall and a silver door next to it and in-between them was a small silver couch and table. There were also some notice boards on the wall behind.

"That's the Head office", Ben told Jonathan as he noticed him looking at the gold door.

"What's up *there*?" Danny asked indicating towards a wide staircase on their right hand side. It had gold railings and was covered in red carpet with coloured swirls on.

"You'll soon find out", Ben smiled, "but first I've got to tell you how the Mirrors work". He walked over towards the right, not far from the bottom of the stairs and pointed to some very tall, gold and black mirrors that were separated into cubicles. There was a metal bar across the top and on it hung a crimson curtain.

"This is how you contact the outside world", Ben told them. They looked at him confused as he explained.

"You should have been given a Mirror Gem", he said. "You place that in here", he went up to one of the mirrors and pointed to a small slot that was the same size as the

Gem at the side of the mirror. "You then turn it and it will glow", he continued. "Close your eyes and think of whom you want to talk to and then they should appear in the mirror. The curtain here is a shield, if you pull it across, no one can hear your conversation".

"Amazing!" Danny beamed.

"Oh, but you can only contact those who are part of the *occult* world. We can't risk mortals finding out about us!"

"Why not?" Danny asked.

Before Ben could answer they heard a very loud roar which came from up the stairs.

They all looked up, horrified at the sudden sound.

"W…what…what was *that*?" Danny asked nervously and stared up into the darkness as Drew hid behind him and peered over his shoulder.

"It's not good", Ben replied frowning.

"What *is* it?" Jonathan asked, looking at him puzzled.

"It's Flame", Ben told them. "It's a *warning!*"

"What's *Flame*?" Danny looked at Ben curiously and then glanced up the staircase.

"He's the Guardian of the Fire Group", he replied.

"*Why* did he make that noise?" Jonathan wondered.

"To let us know that evil has entered the Academy!" Ben looked worried as the four boys stared at each other in horror.

Suddenly Ben bowed down, "Master Vulcane", he said.

Jonathan, Danny, Drew and James looked at him and then up the staircase and were startled when they saw someone walking down towards them. He was a tall, muscular man, with pointy features and had short shaven black hair and a beard. He was dressed in a red jacket with black studs down his chest; the collar on his jacket was turned up. He wore red trousers with a big black belt and big black boots. He watched the boys closely with his cold, grey eyes as he walked slowly towards them.

"It's alright", he told them as he noticed the expression on their faces, his voice was emotionless and cold, "there is no evil here".

"We heard the *call* Master", Ben said, his head still bowed.

"It was a false alarm", Master Vulcane told him, "claims it was a *nightmare*".

"Master", Ben nodded as he walked past them.

"Teach these *rookies* some manners", he said as he walked away.

"What did he just *call* us!?" James said angrily as he glared after him. They watched him go through the silver door and close it behind.

"You're rookies, newcomers, first years", Ben explained. "When you see a Master here, you must bow before them and state their name", he told them.

"I'm not bowing to anyone!" James frowned.

"You *must* James", Ben said turning to look at him sternly. "They're our Masters and it's the rules of The Academy!"

"I'm not calling them *Master!* I'm not a *slave!*"

"No, but we are their *students*, they guide us, help us, we must *respect* them!"

James huffed and folded his arms across his chest, he hated obeying rules.

"You don't want to get into trouble now do ya'?" Ben said looking at him.

James rolled his eyes.

"So where are you taking us next?" Jonathan quickly asked trying to change the subject. He could sense the anger that was about to explode in James.

"Well I could show you the classrooms", Ben replied. "Come on".

They followed him through a set of big silver double doors at the end of the hall which opened into the corridors. The walls were a Midnight blue and the floors had a marbled shiny effect. There were so many doors on either side of them, all silver in colour, some single, some double. They headed towards one of the big double doors in front of them; this had a gold outline and a big clock above it on the wall. They didn't go through though, instead Ben took them to the left, they felt like they were in a big maze with all the twists and turns they took.

"These are all the classrooms", Ben told them as they walked past. "There's more on the other side".

Jonathan, Danny, Drew and James looked at the doors as they went by, "Can we go in?" Danny asked hopefully.

"No, they're being used", Ben told him as he stopped at a big silver double door at the end of the corridor. "Now this", he said smiling, "is where you'll be most likely to find me".

He pushed open the door and led the others inside. The four boys stared in amazement at the enormous swimming pool in front of them. There were dark blue spectator seats all around facing the pool, kind of like being in a big arena.

There was another set of silver double doors at the far end of the room and around the pool were big soft blue plastic mats. There were five people in the pool, four girls and one boy but as the boys got closer they could see that they had no legs, just big colourful tails. They were Mer-people.

Chapter Eight
The Students

THEY STOPPED STILL as Ben and the others entered the room and looked at the newcomers.

"Hi Ben!" one of the girls said smiling as she swam up to the side of the pool. She was very pretty and looked to be the same age as Ben. She had long, straight fair hair which was shaped around her round face, big brown eyes and wore turquoise coloured eye shadow which matched her shimmering tail, bikini top, choker chain and the flower in her hair. She had pearl earrings and had pale pink lips which complimented her fair skin.

"Hi Phoebe", Ben smiled back.

"So who are your *friends*?" she asked looking at Jonathan, Drew, Danny and James who were all looking at her. They'd never seen a mermaid before, nor did they think they even existed.

Ben introduced the boys one by one and told her what they all were as the other Mer-people in the pool swam up.

"Well it's nice to meet you", Phoebe smiled and held out her long pale hand for them to shake. She was wearing a beautiful turquoise bangle around her left wrist.

"Hi!" the boys smiled as they shook her hand one by one, they were still a bit fascinated by her beautiful tail.

"Let me introduce you to my friends", Ben told them and indicated at each of the Mer-people in the pool. "This is Phoebe Johnson". He smiled and nodded towards her. "This is Bridget Butterfield", he said as he waved his hand at a dark-skinned girl who seemed to be younger than the rest. She had brown eyes, and wore her black curly hair in a bob on the top of her head. She was wearing peach col-oured make-up which matched her bikini-top and also wore pearl earrings.

As the boys looked closer they saw that she didn't have a tail like the rest, instead she was wearing the matching bikini bottoms. They looked puzzled and Ben noticed this and explained.

"Bridget's not got her tail yet", he told them smiling. "She's only a *third* year".

Jonathan looked at him, "*when* will she get it?" he asked.

"Next year", he replied. "You undergo your transfor-mation in the fourth year".

"Transformation!?" they all looked at him curiously and a little bit terrified.

"Yeah", Ben smiled at them, they looked worried, "you become *what* you are".

"*What* we are?" Danny gulped.

"Don't look so worried", Ben told them as he noticed their faces. "It's ok, there's nothing to be scared of, you just... get your *features*".

They didn't like the sound of that so Ben quickly told them what to expect. "Jonathan, you'll get your *wings* in the fourth year", he smiled at him. "Drew you'll get *stronger* and be able to *control* your visions. Danny you'll be able to change into *whoever* and *whatever* you want to be, and James your magic will grow more *powerful*".

They looked at each other and then smiled and nodded at Ben, that didn't sound so bad.

"Ok then", Ben turned to look at his friends and continued to introduce them, "this is Jasmine Maitland". Another one of the girls swam up. She was younger than Phoebe and had fair skin and short dark hair which sat perfectly under her chin. She wore a pink and red coloured bikini-top which matched her beautiful tail, choker and headband. She had green eyes and wore dark pink eye shadow and blusher and had bright red lips. Once again she had pearl earrings.

"Hi!" she smiled.

"This is Siobhân Collins", Ben continued as he pointed to the last girl in the pool. She was a very tall; fair skinned girl, about the same age as Jasmine. She had bright blue eyes and short cropped blonde hair and wore pearl earrings, light purple eye shadow both above and under her eyelids and her bikini-top was gold which matched her tail. The boys watched as it gleamed in the pool.

"Finally we have Oli McPartlin", Ben said as he grinned at the only boy in the pool.

He was younger than Ben, tanned, had green eyes and light brown hair which was gelled up at the front and flicked out behind his ears. He was muscular and had a well toned body. His tail was a light blue.

"Alright", he waved at them and they noticed he had blue and white pearls around his left wrist. They also realised that each of them had an orange starfish tattoo on the top of their right arms.

Ben saw them staring and told them that the pearls and tattoos were what made them who they were, that and their tails.

"It's how we *recognise* each other", he smiled and then turned to face his friends. "Well we'd better get going", he said and nodded them farewell.

"Oh, aren't you coming for a swim Ben!?" they heard Phoebe groan as Ben headed towards the door. She sounded very disappointed.

Ben turned around and smiled at her, she looked sad. "Maybe later", he told her. "I've got to show these guys *how* we eat here, it's almost dinner time".

"Well at least come and say goodbye *properly*!" she pleaded as she held her outstretched hand towards him.

Ben sighed and shook his head at Jonathan, Drew, Danny and James. He grinned and then headed back towards the pool. "Stay there", he told them.

They watched as the Mer-people exchanged a quick smile with one another and then glanced at Ben as he neared the pool. There was a twinkle in their eyes. He stretched out his hand to shake Phoebe's hand, and as he did Phoebe grabbed hold of his wrist and pulled him headfirst into the pool. The Mer-people laughed and giggled as Jonathan, Drew, Danny and James gasped as Ben touched the water. He was no longer wearing his clothes for they had been replaced by a big, green and gold shimmering tail. He had a well-toned body with a six-pack, and wore blue and white pearls around both his wrists. Around his neck was a shell on a bright green chain and he too had the same starfish tattoo on the top of his right arm.

The Mer-people crowded around him as he came up from beneath the water. He didn't seem angry at all instead he smiled at each of them in turn.

"Sorry", Phoebe giggled as she wrapped her arms around him.

"You guys", Ben said shaking his head. "You've got to let me go!"

Suddenly they were interrupted by the sound of a very loud bell that made Jonathan, Drew, Danny and James all jump. Was this another warning? They looked at Ben nervously.

"It's alright", he told them as he saw them staring at him. He turned towards his friends, "now you've *really* got to let me go!"

They smiled and moved out away from him so he could swim to the sides. As he pulled his body out of the water and onto the mats he changed back into his white shirt and blue jeans. He wasn't even wet.

"Bye Ben!" They called as he headed back towards the boys who were staring at him open-mouthed. If they didn't believe Ben was a Mer-boy before, they did now.

"Bye guys", he smiled and waved at his friends. "Come on then", he told the others as he walked past them, "stop looking like goldfish and let's get some dinner!"

The boys closed their mouths and followed him out of the pool room.

"*How* did you...?" Jonathan wondered looking at Ben's legs as he walked beside him.

"I transform in *water*", Ben told them, "and when I'm out of it I change back".

"Look, forget about the *tail*!" James interrupted. "That *bell*, should we be worried?"

Ben looked at him and smiled. "No, that's the lunch bell", he told the boys as he led them back through the corridors. "When you hear it you have exactly half an hour to get into the cafeteria, otherwise the doors will close and you won't get any food!"

The four boys looked at each other.

"Don't worry", Ben reassured them, "no matter *where* you are in the Academy you should always make it on time. Here we are". He had returned to the set of big double silver doors opposite the entrance hall, the one with the gold outline around the frame and the big clock above it. The doors were open now. They looked around as Ben led them inside. The room was enormous and had a white tiled floor and was filled with long rectangular beige tables with matching chairs around them. Each of the walls were a different colour. One wall was red, one yellow, one green and the other blue.

"Cool!" Danny smiled as he looked at them.

There were steps either side of a long platform at the far end of the room. There was another table along it, this one was silver and had four seats behind it which over-looked the cafeteria. There was another big clock above it which matched the one outside.

"This is the cafeteria", Ben smiled and led them to a table where they took off their backpacks and sat down op-posite him.

"Where's the *food*?" Danny asked, he looked around puzzled.

Ben smiled. "Watch", he said and he closed his eyes. The four friends watched and then gasped in amazement at the nice, fresh salad with cooked meat that had suddenly appeared in front of him on a silver plate, with matching cutlery on the table along with a Mango and Passion fruit flavoured juice that was in a silver cup. Ben opened his eyes and smiled. "*Believe* and you will *achieve!*" he told them. "That's the motto of the Academy".

Jonathan, Danny, Drew and James all looked at each other and then at Ben. They couldn't believe it.

"Try it", Ben told them smiling.

"How?" Jonathan asked.

"Just close your eyes and *think* about the food you want to eat and it should appear!"

All four of them closed their eyes and thought about it and then they slowly opened their eyes and saw that it had actually worked. They couldn't believe their eyes as they stared at the food that had now appeared in front of them.

"This is so *totally* cool dude!" Danny grinned as he took a bite out of his cheeseburger.

The others agreed as they picked up their food. Jonathan had two salad rolls, Drew had thought up some hot chicken soup, which was in a silver bowl and James was tucking into a bacon buttie with brown sauce.

They enjoyed their food as they watched other students entering the hall, they were all different ages and some were dressed in weird and wonderful clothing and others had tops on that matched the walls. Some of them looked at the newcomers curiously.

Danny thought that his ginger hair didn't stand out so much now as he noticed that some of the other people in the room had a range of different hair colours and styles. One boy he noticed had at least five different colours in his hair and another boy had bright red hair and others had green and pink!

Wow! He thought to himself.

Jonathan noticed the Mer-people walking past smiling at Ben. They had legs now which were covered in skirts, dresses and trousers. Phoebe winked at him as she and the others took a seat at a table across from them.

"That was really mean, what she did", Jonathan whispered to Ben.

"No", he smiled and shook his head; "she was just *being playful*. It's what we do, what us Mer-people *are*. We just want to have some *fun;* it's all part of *the change*".

All of a sudden a girl took a seat next to Ben. "Hi!" she smiled at him. She had long wavy fair hair, blue sparkling eyes and had pale pink make-up on her face. She wore a pale pink long sleeved top which matched her teardrop earrings. She had pink bracelets which she wore on both wrists and had a lead band on her left wrist. Around her neck hung a silver swirl necklace and she wore a long purple skirt, which had swirls on also, and bright pink shoes on her feet.

"Hi Lucy", Ben smiled and gave her a kiss. "Guys", he said as he looked at them, "this is Lucy Matthews, my *girlfriend*!"

"Hi!" she smiled at them timidly.

They smiled back and nodded. "Hi", they said together.

"Oh", Ben suddenly said remembering, "this is for you!" He took the beautiful pink flower from his belt and handed it to Lucy.

"Awwwww, thank you!" Lucy smiled as she took it and gave him a kiss. She placed it on the table and closed her eyes as she wished for her meal. A few seconds later she made the same meal as Ben had appear in front of her. She smiled as she opened her eyes and began to eat her dinner.

"Lucy's half *fairy*, half *Teleporta*", he told the boys. "She's in her final year, like me".

"Don't fairies have *wings*?" James asked looking at Lucy.

"She has them", Ben replied smiling at her; "she can't bring them out in here".

"Why not?" Danny wondered as he licked some ketchup off his top lip.

"Because in the cafeteria, your powers don't work, the magic's *blocked*!"

"Why?" Danny looked at him curiously.

"Health and safety", Ben explained. "It's the only time all the students here come together, you can't have spells flying around!"

The boys looked at the students around them, they couldn't believe that everyone around them was different, that they were all magical beings, there were so many of them! They noticed that the big doors had now closed and that the chairs at the top of the cafeteria were now occupied by four adults, one of which was Master Vulcane.

Sat next to him was a middle-aged man with round features. He had grey curly hair and a full beard, wore silver framed glasses over his dark eyes and was dressed in a dark green long-sleeved shirt, with a brown waistcoat which went over his round belly.

In the other seats were two younger looking women. One was a Hindu woman with long straight dark hair and eyes. She wore yellow eye shadow, had pink lips and cheeks and was dressed in a two-tone yellow sari. The other was a very pretty blonde with long wavy hair, ice blue eyes and dressed in a long flowing blue dress. Dark blue make-up covered her eyes, pink blusher was on her cheeks and her lips were red. She was chatting happily away to the Hindu woman who was sat next to her.

Occasionally all four of them would look down at the students, keeping an eye out for any trouble. They all seemed friendly except for Master Vulcane who was watching everyone like a hawk with his cold eyes.

Ben noticed the boys looking up at them. "They are the Elemental Masters", he told them. They looked at him blankly.

"Each one of them is in charge of the Groups", he said. "Master Vulcane is the Elemental Master of Fire, Master Gebard is the Elemental Master of Earth, Miss Nutshu is the Elemental Master of Air and Miss Nymphina is the Elemental Master of Water".

"Which group are *you* in?" Danny asked him.

"I'm in the Water group", Ben smiled at them. "Miss Nymphina is *my* Master". He looked up towards the blonde who noticed and smiled down at him showing off a beautiful set of perfect white teeth.

"What group will *we* be in?" James asked nervously, he really didn't want to be in the Fire group.

"Well you'll find out when you get your results from Master Arthur", Ben told them. "We'll go there next". He closed his eyes again and wished up a delicious looking trifle, as did Lucy.

"We can have dessert too!?" Danny's eyes lit up and then he closed them and thought up a big slice of chocolate cake.

Ben smiled as Danny took a big mouthful of cake, getting crumbs around his mouth.

Drew giggled and also wished up a dessert and a few seconds later a slice of cherry cake appeared in front of him on a silver plate.

They all sat chatting happily to one another until one o'clock when the doors slowly opened again. Everyone got up and headed towards them as they left the cafeteria.

"Bye Lucy", Ben said as he kissed her goodbye, "I'll see you later". He turned towards Jonathan, Danny, Drew and James, "Come on, let's go and get your results".

They picked up their backpacks and followed him out of the cafeteria as he led them back into the main entrance hall. He went up to the gold coloured door and knocked on it. "Master Arthur", he said, "the rookies are waiting to see you".

Chapter Nine

Master Arthur

"SEND THEM IN", they heard a deep male voice answer, Jonathan thought that he recognised it.

"Yes Master", Ben nodded at the door and then turned to the boys as he indicated for them to follow him in. He opened the door very slowly as Jonathan followed behind.

Drew looked nervous as he got close to Danny who followed Jonathan and then James was behind.

They walked into a small room, which had a soft violet carpet and warm yellow walls. The boys gazed around at the objects around them. Next to the door on the right hand wall was a long white and silver framed mirror and next to that in one of the corners was a large bookcase filled with ancient looking books.

There was a long, black sofa against the right hand wall and above that was the Academy's motto, *"Believe and you will achieve"* it said in big, fancy gold lettering, which matched the frame around it, the i's were dotted with stars.

There were some silver coloured cupboards in the bottom right hand corner which had small padlocks on them. Some unusual mystical looking objects stood on the black shelves on the other side of the room, and in between them was another gold coloured door.

Ben walked up to a large beige coloured desk that faced the door they had just entered. On it was a large crystal ball, a wand, loads of paperwork and on the end stood four small gold figurines. One was a dragon, one was a dolphin, one was a rabbit and the other a bird.

Behind the desk was a table on which sat a computer screen and a keypad and on the other side, in the left hand corner was a locked lid of some kind.

The boys also noticed two very large, tall doors next to the desk, one was white with gold knobs and the other was made of black steel.

"Master Arthur", Ben said bowing down at the desk.

The big gold chair that was placed at the desk spun around and revealed a small man who had silver and grey coloured hair and beard. His eyes were dark blue and were covered by gold-framed glasses.

He was dressed in indigo coloured robes and had a long silver cape, which was covered in gold stars of different sizes. He also wore a gold headpiece, which had four coloured stones in. They were ruby, topaz, emerald and sapphire and matched his long fabric belt that hung below his knees.

"Welcome my boys!" he smiled as he rose from his seat and walked around the desk to greet them.

Jonathan remembered the rules and bowed down before him. "Master Arthur", he said.

Danny and Drew quickly did the same as James frowned at the little man and stood his ground. Master Arthur looked at him for a moment and then smiled.

"We didn't expect you to come through James", he said in his deep voice.

James was a bit taken aback that he knew his name, as were the others and they looked up at Master Arthur.

"Thank you Mr Meyers", Master Arthur said turning towards Ben. "You can put the wand on the desk".

Ben bowed, "Yes Master", he said and took the laser wand from his pocket and placed it onto the desk and then headed back towards the door. He bowed once more before he left the room and left Jonathan, Drew, Danny and James alone with Master Arthur.

"Now", he turned towards the boys who looked at him nervously, "let's get you four cleaned up shall we?"

The four friends looked at each other.

"Mr Jones, would you please follow me", Master Arthur said. "Mr Fletcher, Mr Murray and Mr Darson, please take a seat", he pointed towards the black sofa.

They did as they were told; even James as Jonathan followed Master Arthur to the gold door on the left-hand side of the room. He opened it for Jonathan to go through first. Jonathan looked through it into a corridor and then glanced at his friends who were watching curiously, he then bowed down to Master Arthur and went through the door. Master Arthur followed him through, smiling as he closed the door behind him.

They were in a corridor with a red coloured carpet and as Jonathan headed down it towards another gold coloured door he noticed that he was walking past shelves of empty bottles which had corks in them. He wondered what they were all for.

He stopped as he approached the door. "Please enter", Master Arthur smiled.

"Yes Master", Jonathan said bowing, he felt a bit strange saying it, James was right he did feel a bit like a servant.

Jonathan slowly opened the door, his hands were shaking.

"It's alright Mr Jones", Master Arthur reassured him, "you have nothing to fear. You are safe at this Academy".

Jonathan nodded and then entered the room. He was standing in a small bathroom, with white tiles on the floor and pale blue walls. To his right in the corner was a small cubicle which had a gold curtain pulled across it. It matched the one that was in front of him.

Master Arthur pulled the curtain away to reveal the white and silver bathtub. It was an oblong shaped tub which was the same length as the curtain. On the small shelf at the end of the tub were some toiletries and a towel hung on a silver rail on the left-hand wall.

Jonathan looked at Master Arthur.

"You will undress", he told him as he pointed towards the cubicle, "and then take a nice, relaxing soak in the bath. You will pull the curtain across and use the products on the side".

"Yes Master", Jonathan bowed and headed towards the cubicle. He started to take off his clothes and found it easier to talk to Master Arthur behind the screen.

"It was you wasn't it?" He asked. "The voice in that room, you gave us these objects".

"Yes", he replied as he ran the taps on the bathtub.

"You have been watching us?"

"Not at all".

"Then how do you know our names?" Jonathan asked curiously.

"I have been doing my research", Master Arthur told him. "We were expecting you earlier in the year though Mr Jones".

"Why?"

"You turned thirteen on the 26th April. All magical beings such as yourself should attend the Academy on their *thirteenth* birthday. Hence the saying, *'unlucky for some'*. But being different is not a curse Mr Jones, it is a *blessing*".

Jonathan smiled. He didn't see that Master Arthur was now pouring some kind of pink liquid in the bathtub which caused a lot of steam. He kept an eye on the cubicle as Jonathan continued to undress.

"You may bathe now Mr Jones", he told Jonathan. "I'll be waiting for you outside the door. Remember pull the curtain across…"

"Yes Master", Jonathan answered as he peered from behind the curtain. The door was closed. He was alone. He quickly got into the bathtub, the water was nice and warm, he sighed as he felt the bubbles on his skin. He pulled the curtain across and started to bathe. He didn't notice that as he did, pink vapours started to rise from the water and swirl around in the air above him.

Meanwhile back in the office, James and Drew were watching Danny as he wandered around the room looking at all the objects.

"Hey, this thing has got Ben's name on it!" He exclaimed as he noticed a small silver box like device next to the computer. There were eight names on it and a small red button next to each. He looked at the names; "It's got Lucy's name on it too!" He said. "I wonder what it is?"

"I don't think you should be touching *anything*!" James groaned, he had his arms folded across his chest, he looked angry. "What if he's *watching* us!"

"Oh!" Danny gasped. "Didn't think of that". He went back to sit on the couch next to Drew. "Wonder what Jonny boy's doing in there?" He said as they all looked at the door.

After they had all taken a bath they gathered in Master Arthur's office and stood before him at his desk. He looked at them and smiled.

"Now as it is your first day at the Academy you will be excused from lessons. Please wear your fleeces just for today so that everyone knows you have just arrived and won't make you attend lessons".

"Yes Master", Jonathan, Danny and Drew bowed. James just glared at him.

"James!" Jonathan whispered, frowning at him.

Master Arthur noticed this, "It's alright!" he smiled and looked at James. "You are *angry*. All of this is a big shock to you. You did not want any of it, but one day Mr Darson you will *accept* who you are and be *part* of this Academy".

James frowned at him and narrowed his eyes. He found that very unlikely.

"You four", Master Arthur continued, looking at them all individually, "have a very *special* bond, *a friendship* that has lasted a long time". He shook his head and closed his eyes. "Unfortunately you are all *different*". He opened his eyes and looked at them in turn. "Mr Jones, you are the clever, mature one, the peacemaker, the leader and will fit in well at this Academy. As will you Mr Murray", he said looking at Danny who smiled. "You are optimistic, the joker, the creative one". He looked at Drew next, "Mr Fletcher, you are the kind, shy, sensitive one, who will at first struggle and have trust issues, but with time you will gain confidence and will find yourself. I just hope you choose the right crowd". He looked at Drew more closely. Drew looked at him with a worried look on his face; he didn't understand what he meant by that. He had already got his friends and was pretty certain that he *had* chosen the right crowd.

"Finally Mr Darson", he sighed looking at James who was still frowning, "you are the strong one, the fighter, you are brave, but a little afraid".

"I'm not *scared*!" James spat back.

Master Arthur smiled. "I want you all to *enjoy* your stay here and no matter what happens I want you to keep *hold* of your friendship. It is your most *powerful* gift".

He opened up the top drawer on his desk and pulled out four golden envelopes. "I am sorry for these results", he said as he handed them each an envelope, "but these are the groups in which you belong and will be part of. Please wait outside in the entrance for your group leaders and they will take you to your dormitories".

They all looked at their envelopes and then looked at each other.

"You may go", Master Arthur told them as he held his hand out towards the door, "but I want you to know, you are *safe* here. But please be aware that not all the students and Masters at this Academy will welcome you, some are *different* and do *not* belong".

The boys looked at each other and then Jonathan, Danny and Drew all bowed. "Yes Master", they said and headed towards the door.

Once they were all outside they did as Master Arthur told them and waited. "What do you think he meant when he said that some people here don't belong?" Danny wondered as he looked at Jonathan.

"I'm not sure", he said. "Let's just be careful ok?"

"He means that some freaks here are *evil* and should have been at the *other* Academy!" James announced.

They all gasped as they stared at him, shocked at what he had just said and Jonathan noticed that tears were starting to form in Drew's eyes again.

"No it *doesn't*!" he said quickly, he didn't want Drew to get upset again and be scared. "He just meant that some *people* here act *differently* and everyone here is *good* otherwise they wouldn't be here!" He nodded at Drew to reassure him.

"Well I don't *trust* him!" James frowned as he shoved his thumb over his left shoulder towards Master Arthur's door. "Did you *see* what happened when we took that bath?"

They looked at him curiously.

"Nothing happened", Jonathan said shaking his head in disbelief.

"You all pulled that curtain across, I *didn't*!" he told them looking smug. "You know what I saw, well I saw him open the door just a fraction so he could get his hand through and there was this potion bottle in it, you know like all those ones we saw on the shelf as we went past? And I saw this pink steam or *something* rising up from the water in the bath in which I was sitting and go into the bottle! Then he closed the door again".

They all stared at him and shook their heads; they couldn't believe what he had just said. They didn't want to believe it and Drew looked absolutely petrified.

"It wasn't anything *evil*", Jonathan said to them all, he was still shaking his head.

"So what *was* it then?" James asked frowning at him.

"I don't *know*!" Jonathan frowned back. "But Master Arthur is *good*, he's the Head of this Academy. He *wouldn't* do anything evil to us!"

"So *why* didn't he tell us about it!?" James wondered.

"Look just because I'm the *clever* one, doesn't mean I have *all* the answers!" Jonathan was starting to get annoyed. "I'm sure he had good reason!"

"Dude look, let's just open these up, yeah?" Danny piped up as he waved his gold envelope.

Jonathan nodded. "Yeah, let's find out what group we're in".

They all opened their envelopes wondering what their results were and hoped that they would all be in the same group.

Chapter Ten

Division

"I'M IN THE *Earth* group", Jonathan announced as he read the writing on the sheet of white paper he held in his hand. It had a fancy gold border around the edge and had only a few words on it.

"Welcome to the Academy of Merlin", Danny read out the words on the sheet. *"I hope you enjoy your stay. You are now part of the Air group"*. He looked at Jonathan.

"Water", Drew said quietly.

Jonathan and Danny looked at him. He looked very disappointed and worried. "What group are you in dude?" Danny asked James but he didn't get an answer. He looked up and saw that fear had spread across James's face as he stared open mouthed at the sheet of paper in his hand.

"James?" Jonathan looked up. "What's *wrong*?"

James didn't say anything, as he stood there frozen to the spot. His heart was racing.

Jonathan and Danny walked over to him and looked at the sheet.

"You're in *Fire!*" Danny exclaimed as he read James's result. He knew why his friend looked so scared now. "It's gonna be alright dude", he told him. "It doesn't *mean* anything!"

James looked at him then gasped, "I'm in *Fire!* In his vision", he pointed at Drew, "I get burnt *alive!* It's gonna *happen!*"

Jonathan and Danny looked at each other as Drew started to cry.

"We *won't* let it", Jonathan told James sternly shaking his head as Danny went to hug Drew.

"*How* can you protect me!?" James said sternly shaking his head; "I *can't* escape Fire if I'm in *that* group!"

"We'll *find* a way", Jonathan nodded at him and then turned to Drew and Danny. "We're being split up, but we're still *best friends*, no matter what!"

"Here, here!" Danny agreed. "Come on, *one for all…*" he smiled as he removed his arms from around Drew and placed his hand palm down in the centre of them all again.

The others smiled, *"and all for one!"* They said as they put their hands on top.

"Hope we're not disturbing you!?" they suddenly heard a familiar Irish voice call out. They looked up and saw that Ben was coming down the staircase. He had three other boys with him, who looked to be his age. One of them was a tall, brown-eyed boy who had his black hair in a quiff and had a bit of stubble around his face. He wore a leather jacket, faded blue jeans and a red T-shirt.

Another boy was smaller in size and had short, fair hair, blue eyes and was dressed more smartly than the others. He wore black trousers and a short-sleeved white shirt.

The third boy was different for he had chin-length dark blue hair and green eyes. He had beads around his neck and wrists and was dressed in a striped yellow and purple baggy T-shirt and light blue cropped jeans. He also wore brown sandals and a small gold studded earring in his left ear.

Jonathan, Danny, Drew and James watched as the four older boys came closer. "Hi Ben", Jonathan smiled.

"Hi guys", Ben smiled back and then peered closely at their jackets, as did the other boys. "Ah I see you're with me Drew, in the Water group", Ben told him. "Don't worry I'll look after ya'!"

"Wait a minute, how did you *know* that?!" Jonathan asked curiously.

Ben looked at him and smiled. "Because of the outline on his jacket, it's a dolphin!"

"What!?" They all looked at Drew's jacket and then at their own and they all saw that there was now a small outline of an animal on the top left hand side of their jackets. Each embroidered on in a different coloured thread. There was a green outline of a rabbit on Jonathan's, a blue outline of a dolphin on Drew's, a yellow outline of a bird on Danny's and a red outline of a dragon on James's.

"They're just like the figures on Master Arthur's desk!" Jonathan suddenly realised.

"Yep!" Ben nodded. "They're the *Group Guardians*!"

"You're with me", one of the boys said as he walked up to Jonathan. "I'm Stephen Blossom".

Jonathan looked up at the fair-haired boy who was smiling at him as he held out his hand. Jonathan shook his hand and introduced himself. Stephen seems like a nice, friendly guy, he thought to himself as he smiled back.

"You're in my group kid", the blue-haired boy said as he took a step towards Danny. "I'm Sam, Sam Shortland".

Danny smiled, "Cool *hair* dude! I'm Danny, Danny Murray".

Sam smiled and nodded. It was clear to Ben that they were going to get on.

Finally the dark-haired boy spoke to James. "I'm Jez Everson", he said in an American accent, "and you're in the Fire group with me. I'm your group leader". He stepped closer and whispered in James's ear, "And personally it's the *coolest* group", he winked.

James half-smiled but still didn't want to be in that group for he knew that somehow he would die in a fire.

"Ok", Ben said looking at the boys, "we're gonna take you to your rooms now and show you around so come with us".

Jonathan, Danny, Drew and James followed Ben, Sam, Stephen and Jez up the staircase which was quite dark and only lit with candles. The floor at the top was big and had a shiny marbled floor, white walls and there were two sets of big silver double doors on the left and right hand walls. The one furthest away on the right had four coloured stars on it in red, yellow, green and blue.

"That's *our* room", Ben told them as he noticed them looking at it, "Group Leaders only I'm afraid".

"The other doors lead to more classrooms", Stephen told them, "and if you look up behind you you'll see the star points that each group receive when they do well".

The boys looked at the top of the wall behind them and saw another big clock and below it four big coloured stars, again in red, yellow, green and blue which had different numbers in the centre on them.

"The group with the most points at the end of each term get rewarded", Sam smiled. "Sometimes you get to go to *different* magical places so it's well worth it!"

Jonathan glanced at James smugly and James just rolled his eyes.

"We're winning at the moment!" Stephen smiled at Jonathan and then looked up at the 87 points they had already received.

"To the right you'll see the toilets", Ben told them as he indicated to the two white doors that were next to each other. One said *"Girls"* in pink fancy writing and the other said *"Boys"* in fancy blue writing.

"And what are *they*?" Danny asked curiously as he noticed the four black archways, one in each direction on the floor. They all had a different coloured light moving inside them. The one furthest away had a red light glowing in the archway, the one to their right had a green glow, the one behind next to the staircase was blue and the archway to their left was yellow.

"They're the dormitories", Jez smiled at them. "Unfortunately you can only pass through the door of *your* group".

"Why?" Danny asked.

"It's just a precaution", Ben told him. "Let's get you guys inside yeah?" He reached out and took Drew's hand. "Come on Drew, you're with me".

Drew looked at him and then looked at his friends as each of the other leaders took them to one of the coloured archways. They looked at each other anxiously and then stared at the big archways and the glowing lights.

"Just walk though", the leaders said in sync.

They all took a deep breath and stepped through the archways.

Ben, Sam, Stephen and Jez turned around and looked at each other and then smiled as they too walked through the archways.

Jonathan stared around at the room he had just entered. It was a big room and was filled with nature. He was standing on soft green grass. There were two big trees in the top left-hand corner and also the bottom right. Around the tree on the right were a log, a grey rock and a computer.

There was a large television screen near the other tree and another log for sitting.

To his left he saw some more logs and a big smooth grey rock in the centre acting as a table.

In the top right hand corner he noticed a little hill with a warren on top and a small brown, very cute rabbit was peeping out of the hole.

Next to the hill on the right hand wall was a small green cupboard and up ahead was a set of bright green double doors.

"Welcome to the Earth room", Stephen smiled. "This is a place where you can just chat and relax or work on the computer or just watch TV".

"Wow!" Jonathan gasped as he watched different coloured flowers move all over the walls around him as if they were growing. He hadn't seen anything like it; it was like the walls were *alive*.

"You have nothing to fear Jonathan", Stephen told him, "we're all friends in this group, we're all the same and I think you'll fit in well".

Jonathan looked at him. "What do you mean you're the *same? What* are you?"

"I don't mean we're all the same magical being", Stephen replied, "just that we have similar personalities. I'm a Wizard anyway".

"I'm half wizard too!" Jonathan smiled and then was startled as the rabbit came out of its hole and up to Jonathan. "Hello", it said in a quiet, feminine voice, "my name is Hoppy and I'm the Guardian of the Earth group".

Jonathan looked down at it and was a bit surprised when she spoke, but then realised he wasn't in the human world anymore so anything was possible.

"Hello", he said back and introduced himself.

"I'm here to guide you", Hoppy told him, "and to *protect* you but don't worry you're safe here. No evil can get into this room without me sensing it".

"What about the *other* rooms?" Jonathan asked, he didn't see how this little bunny was going to protect anyone.

"Don't worry Jonathan", Stephen reassured him, "there is an invisible force field all around the Academy so no one from the Dark Academy can get in. The only way anyone can get here is through that building in which you arrived. It's gone now and won't appear again until the next rookies come".

"What about that warning we heard earlier?" he asked curiously.

"That was a false alarm", Hoppy answered. "Flame *must* have been sleeping and had a bad nightmare".

Jonathan nodded. He did feel safe in this room, only it didn't feel like a room with all the nature surrounding him. He felt warm as if the sunlight was bouncing off his face. It was so peaceful too.

"So where will I be sleeping?" he suddenly asked as he looked around. He couldn't see any beds.

"Follow me", Stephen said as he walked straight-ahead leading Jonathan through the double green doors.

"*Awesome dude!*" Danny grinned as he entered the room and stared at the white clouds that were actually moving across the pale blue walls that surrounded him. It was like being in the sky.

The carpet was a pale yellow and the couches on the right hand side of the room were like big, white fluffy clouds. There was a big, wide, yellow table in the centre of them and a large television screen in the top right hand corner.

On his left was a big, tall tree, which had a little yellow bird sitting on a branch. It watched Danny as he gazed around the room.

Next to the tree was a small yellow cupboard and next to that in the top left hand corner was a kind of mini tornado spinning around in the corner on a raised platform.

There was a double set of bright yellow doors ahead of him.

"Welcome to the Air room", Sam smiled. "If you think the walls are cool wait 'til ya' see this!"

Danny watched as Sam walked towards the tornado and gasped as Sam stepped into it. It swirled around him, working its magic and then Sam jumped out and was levitating in the air!

Danny couldn't believe his eyes, Sam was flying!

"Now *this* is cool right!?" He said as he smiled down at Danny who was staring open-mouthed at him.

"Yeah! How did you...?"

"Magic!" Sam winked. "This is the Air Room so we have to fly, go on try it!"

Danny didn't hesitate, he rushed over to the tornado and stepped inside. He could feel the cool air spinning around him and suddenly felt a lot lighter. He stepped out and then leapt up into the air and he too was hovering.

"Totally *cool*!" he beamed.

Sam smiled. He could tell that Danny was going to fit in well with his group.

"Are we having fun!?" Danny heard a beautiful high voice say behind him. He turned around and saw that the little yellow bird was now hovering beside him. He looked at it curiously.

"Did you just…"

"Speak?" the bird said, finishing off Danny's sentence.

Danny stared at it with his mouth open. He couldn't believe that this little yellow bird was actually talking.

"I'm Melody", the bird chirped, "Guardian of the Air group, and *you* are?"

"Danny", Danny answered.

"Hello Danny", she said smiling. "Welcome to the group. If there's anything you need or you just need to talk I'm here for you. I'm here to help, to *guide* you".

Danny turned around and looked at Sam who was now doing the backstroke in mid air. He grinned.

"Thanks, so how do we get *down*?" Danny wondered.

"Just push yourself downwards and touch the floor with your feet", Melody told him as she flew around him.

Danny did as she said and sure enough he was stood firmly back on the floor. "Come on", Sam said, he was already down, "I'll show you to your room".

"Ok", Danny smiled as he followed Sam through the big bright yellow doors.

"This is the Water room Drew", Ben told him as Drew looked around at the room into which he had just entered. It was big and there were bubbles floating upwards across the pale blue walls. He was standing on a dark blue carpet with light blue swirls on. He watched them nervously as they spun slowly like mini whirlpools about to swallow him up.

"It's *cool* isn't it?" Ben smiled as he noticed Drew looking.

Drew didn't say anything but just smiled a little as he took in the rest of the room. In the centre was a big, stone, round fountain and on the left-hand side of that was a big, round hot tub which was bubbling away. There was a television screen on a raised blue platform in the bottom left-hand corner of the room. On the other side of the hot tub in the top left-hand corner was a large; soft looking couch made of light blue rubber with a long white wooden table in front of it. There were more seats and tables on the right hand side of the room, which were in front of a very large aquarium.

Drew looked and saw that there were some rubber steps leading up to it in-between the two couches on his right. There were two small ledges above the couches and doors at the end of them.

"Changing rooms", Ben told him. "If you want to go in the aquarium for a swim. Go up the steps, walk along the ledge, right for girls, left for boys, and go through the door and get changed. Then come out and dive in the pool". He moved his finger along the ledges as he explained.

Drew smiled and nodded and then noticed there was someone in the water, below the surface. It looked like they were talking to a dolphin.

Drew walked over to the glass and peered inside, trying to understand how this girl was able to breathe, for she wasn't wearing any breathing apparatus.

She had short-cropped dark purple hair with black streaks, brown eyes and she wore a black and light purple spotted bikini.

Ben walked over to Drew, "That's Stacey Applebite, fourth year student", he told him. "In this group we can breathe underwater, you don't have to be a Mer-person. She's talking to Finley who is our Group Guardian. Underwater no one can hear you speak, so you can talk in confidence".

Drew just stared through the glass at the dolphin and then at Stacey, he couldn't believe that this was even possible, but then again *anything* was possible at the Academy.

"Now this Drew", Ben said as he walked away from the glass and pointed towards a small blue cupboard that was at the end of the aquarium near a set of double bright blue doors, "this is where you can get your supper if you're feeling a bit peckish".

Drew looked and walked over to Ben who was now kneeling down beside it. "You can get food here and drink from 9:00-11:00pm. It won't open 'til then. All the rooms have one, just open the left-hand door and put your hand in and visualise either milk or hot chocolate". He demonstrated with his hands trying to explain. "Then close that door and open the right-hand door and you can either have cookies for supper or a bag of crisps, then just close it again". He smiled and nodded at Drew to make sure he understood. Drew smiled back timidly and looked at the cupboard.

"Ok then, if you come through here", Ben said next as he opened the set of bright blue double doors that were at the far end of the room, "I'll show you your room".

Drew nodded and nervously followed Ben through the doors and into a long corridor.

James stood in the room and stared in horror at the huge flames that were surrounding him on every wall.

"Cool isn't it!?" Jez smiled.

"Are they *real*?" James asked nervously.

"No, just an illusion", Jez told him, "but they heat up the room making this room warmer than the rest. Looks like *Hell* doesn't it!?" he laughed.

James gulped. He didn't want to be in this room but he looked around carefully.

He was standing on a red marbled shiny floor which had a small volcano in the centre of the room, with a pool of lava around it, enclosed by black iron bars.

James watched as it bubbled and spat out tiny fireballs which disappeared into the air. There was a big screen on his right which had a games console plugged into it and a wide screen television next to it. Facing them were big, soft looking black seats, and against the right hand wall and the top right hand corner of the room were two large, leather couches which had a small, wooden red table in-between them.

There was another large, leather couch against the bottom right hand wall and this one had a long wooden red table in front of it

Next to it against the left hand wall was a small red cupboard. A double set of bright red doors faced him at the far end of the room. To their left was a big cave and inside…

"A *dragon*!" James jumped as he noticed the dragon that was sleeping inside. It had black and dark red scales, a gold undertone with gold plates on its head, along its spine down to its gold tipped pointed tail. It was only the size of a small dog but James still looked frightened as it woke up and gazed at him with its cold, gold eyes.

"Don't be scared James", Jez told him, "it's only Flame".

"Flame!?" James remembered. It was this creature that had made that awful chilling sound before.

"Hello James", Flame grinned, showing of his set of sharp white teeth, "we've been expecting you". Its voice was a low growl.

James stared at him nervously and gulped.

"I'm going to guide you", Flame told him, there was a twinkle in his eyes as he came closer.

"Flame is our Group Guardian", Jez told James. "You can talk to him about anything, or me or Master Vulcane. He's our Master, in charge of the Fire group. We're all here to help you settle in".

"I don't want to settle in!" James snapped. "I don't want to be any part of *this freak show*!"

Jez stared at him in disbelief but Flame just smiled. "Don't worry James", he said, "you're gonna fit in here just fine!"

James glared at him.

"You might not want to be here *now* James", Jez said as he looked at him, "but with time you *will*. You will be one of us!"

"I doubt it!" James spat back.

"You have fire in your soul", Jez told him, "just like the rest of us in this group. This is where you *belong*".

James shook his head, frowning at Jez who then walked over to the set of bright red double doors and opened them.

"Come on", he said, "I'll show you where you will be sleeping".

Chapter Eleven
Friend Or Foe?

ALL THE BOYS had walked into a long corridor, which had doors on either side in their group colours. The walls were black and the floor was marbled.

"These are the dormitories", the leaders told them. "The doors on the left are the boy's rooms and the doors on the right are the girl's rooms".

Jonathan saw that there were more girls in this group than boys as there were only four doors on the left and six doors on the right.

There were also more girls in the Air and Water groups as both had more doors on the right than the left but in the Fire group, boys were more dominant.

"The doors at the end are the bathrooms", the leaders told them, "and this room", they said as they headed towards a big gold coloured door at the end of the corridor, "this is *whatever* you want it to be!" They smiled as the boys looked at them curiously.

"Come and see", they said as they slowly opened the door and stepped inside a large white covered room that didn't have any windows. They closed the doors behind them as the newcomers looked around curiously.

"This is a room where you can just escape to, all you have to do is close your eyes and think about the place you wanna be".

Jonathan, Danny, Drew and James all watched as the leaders closed their eyes and suddenly the room changed around them.

"Totally *cool* dude!" Danny grinned. They were at the beach, no longer in that room, but the door was still where it was before.

Sam opened his eyes and smiled. "It's amazing isn't it!? It can be anything you want it to be Danny, try it".

Danny closed his eyes and thought about a place he would like to be, he got a really strong visual image in his head and slowly opened his eyes. It had worked. They were amongst the stars. They were in space.

"Awesome!" Danny beamed.

"When you touch the handle of the door the place disappears so no one can see where you went and what you were doing", Sam explained. "You have complete *privacy* here". He touched the handle and sure enough the room was back to normal.

"Come on", he said as he held the door open for Danny, "I'll give you a quick glimpse of the bathroom now and then show you to your room".

All of the boys followed their leaders out and then walked into the bathrooms as the leaders held the doors open for them.

The bathrooms all looked the same in the boy's bathroom, they were big and had white tiled floors, pale blue walls and four tall mirrors on the wall at the far end framed with silver. There were four white basins in front of each with a small blue tub in-between the silver taps. Either side of the mirrors were two light blue coloured doors.

There were two large white bathtubs either side of the room and each had a little, dark blue shelf full of toiletries and a soft, dark blue towel hung from a silver rail on the wall near each bathtub.

A long dark blue curtain hung on another silver rail which separated the tubs and hid them from view.

The leaders entered the bathroom. "Everyone in this group uses this room", they said. "Walk up to the mirrors, look in and your bathroom essentials will appear. You use a towel; another will replace it, same as the toiletries".

"Cool!" Danny smiled; he loved being surrounded by all this magic.

"The doors over there and there", the leaders said pointing to the light blue coloured doors, "are the toilets. So that's the bathroom, now for the dormitories".

They headed back towards the door and the boys followed them back out into the corridor.

"This is where you will be sleeping", they said as they opened one of the doors on the left and nodded for them to go inside.

The dormitories were large, and the walls and carpets were different shades of their group colours, as were the sheets and duvets on the four beds, two either side of the room. Next to them was a small wooden set of drawers, which had tiny keyholes instead of knobs and a black alarm clock on top of them.

At the far end of the room was a long wooden desk which had a black lamp on it.

A soft black chair faced the wall at the desk. Above it were four silver lockers and two small windows were either side.

Next to the door on the left-hand wall was a tall mirror framed in gold and on the other side of the door was a strange looking white cubicle.

"That is your Transformation Cove", the leaders told the boys as they all looked at it wondering what it was. "Just step inside and state what you are and you're ready for class".

None of them understood, so the leaders showed them as they stepped inside the cove.

"Telekinetic", Jez said out loud and the cove lit up. James had to shield his eyes as the light was so blinding. As he moved his arm away from his face he saw that Jez was now dressed head to toe in black leather. His jacket had a silver stripe down the left-hand side of his chest and had a small silver stud on his jacket collar which was

wrapped tightly around his neck. Around his waist was a black belt with silver studs all around it and his trainers were black with silver laces and soles.

James stared at him.

"This is what a sixth year Telekinetic will dress like", he smiled, "and if you want to change back just state your name, your full name. *Jeremy Everson*", he said and the cove lit up again and he was back in the clothes he was wearing before.

"If you have a free period, you just state your name also and you'll be dressed in whatever is *you*", the leaders said. "When it's time for bed, just say *bedtime* and you'll be in what you usually wear or what you want to wear".

They smiled at the boys, "So that's it, tour over".

"If there's anything you need, or just need to talk then feel free to knock on our door", Stephen said smiling at Jonathan. "You can talk to either me, or Hoppy or even Master Gebard, Master of our group. You've seen the Elemental Masters room right? Next to Master Arthur's in the main entrance?"

"Yes", Jonathan nodded. "Thank you". He looked at the beds. "Which one is mine?"

"Oh right, sorry", apologised Stephen, "this one". He pointed to the bed on the left, next to the mirror in the bottom left hand corner of the room. "You'll be sharing with Calumn, Carl and Milo. Calumn and Milo are also first years and Carl is in the second year. I think you'll get on well with them".

Jonathan nodded and put down his backpack.

"Oh yeah and you can put your stuff in the drawers or lockers", Stephen told him. "You have a key so that way you can keep all your personal belongings safe and no-one can take them".

All the boys put their bags in their lockers and kept the small golden keys in their pockets.

"Don't lose it!" Sam told Danny. "I'm putting you with Joey, Sky and Luke. Joey's a Metamorph like you, Sky's a Nymph and Luke is half Wizard and half Fairy".

"Cool!" Danny grinned.

"That's your bed", he told him as he pointed to the bed in the bottom right hand corner of the room next to the Cove.

Danny nodded excitedly at Sam.

"I've got to go now, as I have a class", Sam told him. "You'll be alright now won't ya'?"

"Sure thing dude!" Danny gave Sam a thumbs up and watched as he walked over to the Transformation Cove and stated what he was. "Genie", he said loudly.

Danny's eyes lit up; "You're a *Genie*!?" he smiled as he looked at the clothes Sam was now wearing. He was in a light blue and gold waistcoat type of jacket which showed off his well-toned tanned body to good effect. He wore matching pantaloons with a gold silk belt hanging from his waist and also a matching headpiece with gold jewels inside. There were gold cuffs around his wrists and he wore gold pointed fabricated shoes.

"Yep! Your wish is my command!" Sam laughed.

Danny laughed too and then watched as he left the room, leaving Danny all alone.

"This is your bed Drew", Ben said as he pointed to the bed in the top left-hand corner of the room, next to the window. "Your roommates are Josh Jacobs, Adam Bennett and Rob Fuller. They're alright; they'll look after you".

Drew didn't want to share a room with strangers; he wanted to be with his friends. Ben could sense the fear and tried to reassure him.

"It's going to be ok Drew, you're safe here, don't be scared ok? You'll make some new friends. We're all friends in this group, we look out for one another. We want you to fit in".

Drew was unsure and just gave a quick smile, but kept his head down.

Ben looked at him and smiled, he could see that trying to make Drew become part of his group was going to be difficult.

"Let's go and find your friends shall we?" he said and Drew looked up at him then and smiled.

"Yeah", he nodded and they left the room.

"I'm sorry to put you in this room James", Jez told him, "but it was the only one with a vacant bed". He pointed to the bed in the top right hand corner of the room, next to the Cove. "They're not gonna like it, but don't worry they can't hurt you, you don't need to be scared".

"I'm *not* scared!" James frowned at him.

"Well that's good", Jez smiled. "If you need to talk to me, or Flame or even Master Vulcane, just come and find us, if they do anything to ya' just let us know and we'll try and sort it, ok?"

"Whatever!" James huffed as he folded his arms across his chest and rolled his eyes.

"Ok then, just be *careful*", Jez warned, "and be sure to read the Rulebook, the rules must be *obeyed*, even though some students here, including your roommates think it's *fun* to break one or two".

"Yeah *whatever!*" James said shaking his head, so he was going to be sharing this room with some rule breakers. No big deal, he could handle that he thought to himself.

Jez looked at him. "I'm gonna go now, see ya' around James", he said and he left the room as James stared angrily after him.

Ben and Drew saw Danny as they emerged from the blue light of the archway and Drew smiled, happy to see his best friend.

"Hey Drew!" Danny grinned and waved. "Like your room?"

"Yeah", Drew nodded.

"So are you kids going to be ok now?" Ben asked. "If I were you I'd try and find your classrooms, you don't want to be late for your classes tomorrow, not on your first day".

Danny nodded, "Yeah, we'll go exploring, come on Drew let's get our time tables and see where we need to be. Thanks for the tour Ben".

Ben smiled as Danny went back into the yellow light and he watched as Drew tried to follow him through but a force field blocked him. He stepped back in shock.

"You can't go through Drew remember?" Ben told him, "only students in the *same* group".

Drew nodded and then put his head down as he walked past Ben and back into the Water room.

Jez came out of the Fire room and looked at Ben as he walked up to him. "How's James?" he asked.

"Moody", Jez replied. "He doesn't want to fit in. We're gonna have problems with this one. I've had to put him with Hart's gang".

"Is that wise?"

"It was the only bed left, he'll be fine. They're only *third* years anyway".

"And what about next year?"

"He should be part of this group", Jez smiled.

"As long as he's not one of *them*!" Ben warned him.

"I'll report back to Master Vulcane if they touch him", Jez replied. "He'll deal with them".

Ben nodded, "I'm going to have problems with Drew too, he's too shy, he's scared, and he has no idea what he's capable of".

They stopped talking as Danny emerged from the Air room and waited for Drew. "Take Care Danny, please tell Drew that everything will be fine", Ben said and then nodded his head towards the leaders room as he looked at Jez who nodded and followed him through.

Danny watched as they closed the door behind them and Drew stepped out from the blue light of the archway.

Jonathan was exploring the Academy and trying to find his classrooms. He walked down a long corridor and came to a large set of double silver-framed doors on the left hand wall. He peered inside the two long rectangular windows on the doors. It was a kind of cloakroom and there were a few bags on the light purple coloured carpet. He opened the door and went through. There was another big door in front of him. He walked up to it and peered through again and saw that this room was full of wooden shelves containing books. He had found the Library.

The Library was very big and had lilac coloured walls, and a grey carpet. He went through and looked around at the ten wooden tables that were scattered in the room and had purple velvet chairs around them. There were some students sitting in some of the chairs reading books. Some looked up at him as he entered.

There was a big white desk next to the doors on his right, which had a computer on it and some drawers full of files and other paperwork behind it. At the desk, in a soft purple velvet swivel chair sat a tall, bald headed man with a greyish silver beard who wore silver framed glasses over his bright blue eyes and was dressed smartly in a brown waistcoat with matching trousers and a short-sleeved white shirt.

He must be the Librarian, Jonathan thought to himself as he continued looking around the room.

To his right, at the far end of the room was a long row of eight computers. Purple swivel chairs were at the table on which they stood, facing the screens.

Jonathan smiled and walked around the bookshelves looking at the books that caught his interest. He was going to like it here.

He picked up a book and noticed it had a coloured sticker on, he saw that they all did, some were different colours. They were in white, yellow, green, blue, orange and red. He looked at them and wondered what it meant.

He came to a set of stairs that led to a small black door and there was a clocking device next to it on the wall. He went up and took his Library card from his pocket and swiped it. Nothing happened. He looked at his card puzzled and tried again. Still nothing. He didn't understand, why wasn't it working?

"What colour is your card?" he heard a quiet, voice say in a Californian accent. It made him jump. He looked down and saw that there was a tall boy sitting at one of the tables.

He was looking up at him with his big brown eyes. He had light brown floppy hair and was wearing a green and blue checked short sleeved shirt, and blue combat trousers, which matched the cuffs he wore around his wrists.

"It's white", Jonathan told him as he held up his card to the boy. He looked to be the same age as Jonathan.

"It won't work then", the boy whispered. "It's a restricted area, only fifth and sixth years are allowed through".

Jonathan nodded as he came down the stairs. He watched as the boy got up from his seat and met him at the bottom.

"I'm Milo Lee", he said holding out his hand.

"Oh", Jonathan said looking surprised, "you're my roommate. I'm Jonathan Jones. Pleased to meet you". He shook Milo's hand and smiled.

"Likewise", Milo smiled back. "So what kind of magical being are you?"

Jonathan told him and then asked Milo what *he* was.

"I'm a Mimiko", he told him.

"What's that?" Jonathan asked, he had never heard of that before.

"Well from what I've read", Milo said pointing towards the book which was opened on the table, "a Mimiko is a creature who can copy the powers of others".

"That's cool", Jonathan nodded.

"Yeah it is", Milo agreed, "so do you know about the colour code here?" he asked.

"No", Jonathan said shaking his head and Milo explained that they were only allowed to read books with white stickers which matched their cards.

"Try opening one of the other books, with a different coloured sticker on", he suggested.

Jonathan took a random book off the shelf behind Milo; it had a tiny blue sticker on in the top right hand corner. He went to open it, but couldn't. It was like the pages had been glued together. He looked at the book puzzled.

"That's a book for fourth years", Milo told him. "My theory is that the contents of the books that are magically bound will tell us more about advanced magic. They may contain *dangerous* information and spells, darker magic that we're not supposed to know about yet".

"You could be right", agreed Jonathan and looked up at the black door. "It's the same through there isn't it? That's why it's restricted".

Milo nodded, "Think so".

Jonathan looked at some of the other books on the shelf. *"So you're about to change"*, he read out one of the titles with an orange sticker on it.

"You know about the transformations here?" Milo asked him as he looked nervously at the book Jonathan held in his hand. "In the fifth year, students *change*. They undergo a *transformation*, become what they are *meant* to be and…" he paused, "they're not afraid anymore, they just *accept* it".

Jonathan looked at him and then at some of the other students in the Library. Some of them were quietly reading at the tables whilst others were sitting at the computers. He wondered if any of them had undergone a transformation yet.

"Have you read the Rulebook?" Milo whispered.

Jonathan shook his head. "Not yet", he replied.

"Go and ask Robert if you can have a copy", he said as he pointed to the man in the chair who was typing away on the computer. "Some of the rules, well they don't sound too great".

Jonathan wondered what he meant so he put the book back which he had in his hand and walked up to the Librarian and asked politely for a copy of the Rulebook.

Robert peered over his glasses at Jonathan and gave a warm friendly smile.

"You must be new to the Academy", he said as he got up from his chair and walked over to where Jonathan was standing. "Welcome, I trust you have been given a card?"

"Yes Master", Jonathan bowed.

"Oh, no dear boy you don't need to bow", the Librarian told him. "I'm not a Master here, just the Librarian. A Wizard, but you can call me Robert".

"Sorry", Jonathan apologised.

"That's quite alright, now as a first year you are only allowed to look at the books with white stickers and if you want to take them out, bring them to me and I'll stamp them for you. They must be brought back within two weeks mind", he told him.

Jonathan nodded to show that he understood.

"You can use the computers anytime, just swipe your card along the bottom of the screen and you'll be asked for a password, anything you want. Once you type it in the system will remember it and log you onto the Internet for next time".

Jonathan nodded again as Robert smiled and handed over the Rulebook from behind his desk.

"Remember the rules *must* be obeyed", he told him, "and I'm sure you know the number one rule for the Library?"

Jonathan thought for a moment. "To be *quiet*", he answered.

Robert smiled, "That is correct. You may talk, but please do it quietly otherwise I may be forced to use *this*", he said as he produced a long black wand from behind his desk. It had a small gold star on its tip.

"I will", Jonathan nodded. "You won't get trouble from me. Thank you for the Book", he said and walked away back to where Milo was sitting at a small table and looked at the Rulebook. It was just the same as the book in his backpack, a black cover with a gold star emblem surrounded by a circle which had a triangle in its centre on the front. It must be the Academy's logo Jonathan thought to himself.

He opened it up as Milo watched him and started reading the rules and was shocked at what he read.

Jonathan and Milo went to the cafeteria when they heard the bell at 6:00 and they met up with Danny, Drew and James. Jonathan introduced them to his new friend.

"Pleased to meet all of you", Milo smiled and shook Danny and Drew's hand but James just looked at him suspiciously.

"What's your problem?" Milo asked, "I'm only *being friendly!*"

"Don't mind James", Jonathan told him, "he's the *moody* one, doesn't want to be any part of this, has *trust* issues".

James huffed as he frowned at Jonathan.

"Well wait until you get to be a fifth year, then you'll be part of this Academy whether you want to be or not", Milo told him.

James looked at him. "I don't even know if I'm gonna make it to *fifth* year!" he moaned and glanced at Drew.

Milo looked puzzled so Jonathan explained about Drew's vision as they ate their meals.

"So have you guys met *your* roommates yet?" Milo asked after he had been filled in, he wanted to quickly change the subject.

Danny and Drew shook their head.

"Don't know, don't care!" James said fiercely as he cut away angrily at his steak pie.

Milo watched him, "You're in the *Fire* group", he said.

James looked up at him, "How did you *know*!?" he asked frowning.

"You have *anger* inside, it's bubbling away, you have a strong sense of *hatred*, you want to rebel, let it all out".

James narrowed his eyes, Milo was right; he just wanted to get away from here and scream.

"You must *obey* the rules here James, otherwise you will be banished, *never* to return home!"

Danny and Drew looked at each other nervously as James stared at Milo. "Have you not read the Rulebook?"

They all shook their heads and so Milo bent down, un-zipped his bag and brought his Rulebook out onto the table. He read out the rules as the others listened, horrified at what they heard.

Rule no. 1: No *killing* or *turning* another student.

Rule no. 2: No *Biting* or *feeding* off another student.

Rule no. 3: No using powers *against* or *on* another student.

Rule no. 4: *All* students must retreat to their dormitories by 11:00pm and all doors *must* be shut *especially* at midnight.

Rule no. 5: The use of dark magic is *forbidden*, any student caught using it will be banished to the Spirit Realm for *eternity*. If dark magic is to be used in the criteria then an *authorised* slip by that Master *must* be shown.

Rule no. 6: Students who are intending on going out to the town

must *inform* Master Arthur and wear
the amulet at *all* times whilst out.

Rule no. 7: If under any
circumstance a student should
encounter a student from *The Dark
Academy* whilst in education your
powers must *not* be used against
them *unless* they are a threat.

Rule no. 8: Students must *not*
affect the outcome of their destiny,
the balance between good and evil
must be kept at this Academy.

Rule no. 9: Fifth and Sixth year
students must *not* inform students
below them about what the *future*
holds for other magical beings.

Rule no. 10: *All* students must
show *respect* to the Masters at this
Academy and *bow* down before them,
stating their name.

Milo looked up after reading out the last rule and saw
four white faces staring at the book; even James looked a
bit concerned.

"No *b…biting!?* No *feeding* off another student!? No *t…t…turning* another student!?" Danny spluttered, "What *kind* of a place is this!?"

"Why would they have rules like *that*!?" Jonathan wondered still staring at the book.

"Well", Milo whispered, the others got closer, "when I first arrived a few weeks ago, Master Arthur told me that *some* of the students and Masters here didn't *belong…*"

"He told us that *too!*" Jonathan interrupted. "Sorry go on".

"Well my theory is", Milo continued, "that some of them took the *wrong* path!"

James smiled. He was right all along, and now Jonathan, Danny and Drew realised it too.

"You mean they were meant for *The Dark Academy*", Jonathan whispered. Milo nodded.

"Some of the students and Masters here are *evil!?*" Danny said looking shocked.

"Maybe", Milo said and looked over his shoulder at a table of leather clad boys that were sitting at the far table laughing.

"Are *they* evil!?" Danny asked as he saw where Milo was looking. The others looked too at the table of six boys. Some looked older than the others did.

Milo turned away and faced his friends, "Well they call themselves *Bad Boyz*", he told them in a low whisper.

"What are they?" Jonathan asked.

"Don't know but they're not Mimikoes".

They turned to look at him. "You should be *careful* James", he warned, "they're in the *Fire* group, in fact a lot of them are, the ones who have a *darkness* inside".

"I'm not scared of *them*!" James said frowning in their direction. One of the boys on the table caught him looking and gave him an evil, moody stare. He was quite tall, slim built and had short whitish/blond hair, ice blue eyes and dark eyebrows.

James quickly turned away.

"So are some of the Masters here gonna teach us how to be *evil*!?" Danny gulped.

"Maybe, if that's what you're *meant* to be", Milo responded.

"I *don't* want to be evil!" Drew cried.

"Don't worry Drew", Jonathan said trying to comfort his sensitive friend, "I'm sure that *no one* at this Academy is evil. If they were, *why* would Master Arthur enroll them!?"

Milo shrugged and shook his head, "It was only a *theory*", he said looking at Drew. "I didn't mean to upset anybody".

"It's ok", Jonathan told him, "Drew's just a little scared. We all are. Especially after hearing those *rules*!"

Milo apologised and quickly tried to change the subject. "You guys know about the times the cafeteria opens don't you?" He turned a page in his Rulebook and read out the times.

The doors to the cafeteria will open at the following times, students have exactly half an hour to get inside before the doors close, make sure you get there in time or your meal time will be lost.

Breakfast-9:00-9:30
Dinner-12:00-1:00
Tea-6:00-7:00

When the doors open at the end of the meals all students must leave the hall immediately. Any student caught left inside will be severely punished.

"That's a bit harsh isn't it!?" Danny said looking worried.

"You better *obey* the rules then!" Milo told him, the others looked at James. "I'm guessing that they don't give us just *lines* here!"

"I dread to think *what* the punishment is!" Jonathan said looking at the book and then at James. "We *are* going to obey the rules here aren't we!?"

James rolled his eyes, *"Fine!"* he grumbled.

"So what else is in there?" Danny quickly asked looking at the book curiously.

Milo turned the next page, "It's got the list of the clubs that you could join during your free periods", he told him and read them out.

The Social clubs at the Academy
are as follows:

Swimming
Basketball
Athletics
Dance
Motorcycling
Art
Bowling

Any student wishing to join a group
and earn stars for their group must
put their name down on the board
outside the main entrance and speak
to the Team leader of that club where
they will be given a trial run.

If you wish to leave a club
then your name must be
removed from the board.

"They do an *Art* Club!" Danny's face lit up. "I'm signing up!"

"I don't think we should be joining any groups just yet", Jonathan told him. "Let's just settle in first ok?"

Danny nodded, "So are you in any club Milo?"

Milo shook his head, "No but Athletics sound good, I may join that one".

Just then the bell sounded and the doors of the cafeteria slowly opened prompting everyone to get up from their seats and head towards them. The boys waited until some of the aisles had cleared before they too got up and headed out. There were so many students that they didn't want to get crushed in the crowds.

"So where to now?" Danny asked as they walked into the main entrance.

"Well I have a class", Milo told them, "so I'll see you later Jonathan. It was nice to meet the rest of you".

"Wait a minute, it's 7:00pm! You have a class *now*!?" Danny asked.

"Some magical beings have night classes", Milo explained and then waved them all goodbye.

Jonathan, Danny, Drew and James all watched as Milo ran up the staircase, and then Danny pulled Jonathan to one side so Drew wouldn't hear.

"Well he *seems* nice enough", he whispered to Jonathan. "But if what he says is *true* about some of the students here being *evil*, then how can we be sure that he's not one of *them*!?"

"Don't be *stupid*!" Jonathan whispered back.

"I'm not!" Danny frowned. "We don't know what *kind* of being Mimikoes are. I haven't even heard of them!"

"He's alright. Anyway he said that most of them are in the *Fire* group. He's in *Earth* with me!"

"Yeah *most* of them, which means *some* of them are in different groups!"

"He's *not* evil Danny!" Jonathan told him. "Anyway what happened to you!? You got *trust* issues all of a sudden!?"

"I'm sorry", Danny said shaking his head. "It's just, we've already been split up into *different* groups and now you're making *new* friends! Remember what Master Arthur said, that *our friendship* is our most *powerful* gift and that we should keep *hold* of it!"

"I remember", Jonathan nodded, "but I don't think Milo is going to come in-between us". He walked back over to James and Drew who were watching them curiously.

"What you been talking about?" James frowned as Danny came back over.

"Just that we're not going to let anyone destroy this friendship", Jonathan told him and looked at them all as they huddled together. "We took an *oath* many years ago that we would *always* be *best friends* no matter what and that's not going to change even though we've been put into different groups. We will make *new* friends and fit in here but *our* friendship will always remain *strong. No one* will come between us!"

The other three nodded as they remembered when they had met for the first time at Primary school and the happy memories that they had shared.

Chapter Twelve

Roommates

THAT NIGHT DANNY still had Jonathan's words ringing in his ears as he sat on one of the cloud like couches in the Air room. He watched the other students around him wondering which of them were his roommates and hoped that they weren't the wrong kind. They all seemed like nice, friendly people as they laughed and chatted away with their groups of friends. Danny decided it was time to mingle, to fit in, so he got up and talked to anyone who would listen and before long he too was laughing away with a group of boys.

Jonathan and Milo were also chatting. They sat on their beds in their dormitory and got to know each other a little bit better and Jonathan was introduced to the other boys in that room.

Calumn Key was a Metamorph the same as Danny. He had short brown hair, green eyes and dressed in some green and white striped pyjamas.

The other roommate was called Carl Bloom who was a Genie. He had brown spiky hair, which was gelled up at the front; brown eyes and was dressed in a pair of blue pyjamas.

All of Jonathan's roommates seemed like nice people, he didn't see how *any* of them or anyone else in that group could possibly be evil.

Drew and James on the other hand didn't feel like making any new friends as they sat by themselves in the corners of their rooms. They felt like outsiders as they nervously watched the other students around them.

Drew felt really intimidated being surrounded by so many people, people he didn't know and didn't feel very comfortable to be around so he decided to just go to bed.

When he opened the door to his room he saw that there was another student already in there reading a book on his bed in the top right hand corner of the room. He looked up as Drew walked in. He had a long indigo coloured fringe and floppy hair which fell over one of his bright blue eyes and he wore red glasses. He was dressed in a black T-shirt and blue jeans.

Drew smiled a bit and then quickly turned to get into his bed as the boy just looked at him and then carried on reading.

Suddenly the door opened again and a tall, slim built, dark haired boy with blue eyes entered the room. He was wearing black jeans and a blue and white long sleeved T-shirt top with a white star on the front.

"Y'alright!" he said in a Manchurian accent and walked over to Drew's bed. "You're new aren't ya'!?" he asked. "I'm Rob".

Drew pulled the covers back and looked at him nervously, Rob was smiling. "So who are *you*?" Rob asked.

Drew told him his name.

"You're *shy!*" Rob grinned. "Don't worry I'll take good care of ya'! I'll be your *guardian angel!*"

Drew smiled a bit, he wasn't sure whether he liked Rob or not, he was the complete opposite to Drew.

The door opened again then and the third roommate entered the room. He was older than the other boys, tall with short spiky brown hair and brown eyes. He was dressed in blue jeans, a white vest top and a pale blue shirt.

"Alright Josh", Rob said as he entered, the boy looked at him and then noticed Drew.

"Alright Rob", he said smiling. "So who's this then?"

Drew felt nervous again, he didn't like people looking at him.

Rob introduced him to Josh who just nodded and then stepped into the Transformation Cove and changed into his nightwear.

"That's Josh", Rob told Drew. "He's a fourth year and both he and Adam", he nodded towards the boy reading, who glanced at him as his name was mentioned, "are *Spirits*!"

Drew didn't know if this was a good thing or not and watched as Josh got into his bed.

"I'm a half-breed", Rob continued. "Half *angel* and half *god*!"

Drew looked at him. He actually felt safe having an angel as his roommate and gave a timid smile at Rob and then put his head down again.

"So *what* are you then?"

Drew told him.

"A Seer!? Hey, well don't keep us up all night with your visions now will ya'!?" Rob smiled.

"Keep the volume *down* Rob", they heard Josh say from his bed, "some of us are trying to *sleep*!"

"Sorry", Rob whispered. "Goodnight then".

Drew looked up at the door then as he suddenly heard a familiar Irish accent call out *"Lights out"*, and then heard the shuffling of feet as the other students in the group made their way to their dormitories.

"Nite then Drew", Rob said as he switched off the light.

"Nite", Drew said quietly as he pulled the covers back over his body and tried to go to sleep.

James lay in his bed, alone in the darkness underneath his blankets. He opened his eyes as he heard someone enter the room.

"What's *this*!?" he heard a low cold voice say as they noticed the lump that was James under the covers. "We've got ourselves a *roomy* boys".

He heard two other boys laugh maliciously.

"Show *yourself*!" the cold voice demanded, he seemed to be the leader of this group.

James didn't want to see what kind of freaks he was sharing a room with so kept still and made out he was asleep.

"He's *scared* boys!" the cold voiced leader laughed. The other boys laughed too.

James didn't like being laughed at and flung the covers back forcefully and sat up in his bed and looked at the boys in the room. He looked a bit shocked as he recognised their faces.

The boy in the middle had short whitish blond hair and ice blue eyes, the boy on his right was dark-skinned with braided dark hair and big brown eyes and the boy on the left had floppy fair hair and bright green eyes. Unlike his friends he wore a white T-shirt whereas the other boys shirts were black. They all had spiky collars around their necks and dressed head to toe in black leather. The *Bad Boyz*.

They stared at James and he stared back, now that he was over the shock. "So are you a *full* breed kid?" the leader asked him.

James didn't know what he meant by that and just frowned at him. The boy smiled. "Oh where are my manners", he said sarcastically. "We've not introduced ourselves. I'm Jensen Black, this is Bradley Tyson", he thumbed towards the black boy on his right, "and this is Luke James", he thumbed the other boy on his left.

James looked at them all and didn't say a thing; he didn't want to be friends with any of them.

"So *who* and *what* are you?" Jensen asked.

James still didn't speak as he narrowed his eyes.

Jensen smirked, "Not talking huh, well I guess we'll just have to *make* ya'!"

Bradley and Luke both laughed until Jensen held up his hand and they stopped abruptly as if Jensen was controlling them.

"You're *scared* of us!" Jensen grinned.

"No I'm *not*!" James snapped.

"Then tell us *who* and *what* you are!", Jensen demanded.

James didn't like being told what to do and he gave Jensen a disgusted look but he didn't want them thinking he was scared so he told them.

"Well we've got ourselves a *Witch* boys", Jensen said glancing at the other two, "but still, he's a *full* breed like us!"

"Maybe he'll be one of *us* one day, hey Jense!?" Bradley laughed and Jensen and Luke did too.

"No I *won't*!" James said angrily.

Jensen looked at him. "I think you'll fit in *well* here James", he grinned. "We're gonna take *very* good care of you!"

They all laughed again. James found this very unnerving.

"We're *third* years", Jensen told him, "and we all have a very *special* talent". He placed his hand on his chest; "I'm super *strong!*" he smiled wickedly.

"I'm a very good *tracker*", Bradley also grinned.

"And I have super *hearing!*" Luke said, his voice was more gentle than the others.

"We'll develop more abilities as we get older", Jensen grinned, "and that's when the real *fun* will start!" They all laughed.

"Only we're *not* gonna get older are we boys! Not after graduation anyway!" Jensen laughed again louder this time as the other two joined in.

A shiver ran down James's spine as he looked at them curiously, he didn't get the joke.

"We're rivals with *another* gang of our kind", Jensen said after they had stopped laughing. "They dress how *our* kind did in times gone by, one look at them and you can tell what they *are*, but we think the *modern* look is much *cooler*, don't ya' think!?" He tugged on the raised collar of his leather jacket.

"I guess", James shrugged.

"Makes us less *conspicuous*", Jensen grinned.

James had had enough of them being cryptic, they had demanded to know what *he* was and now he wanted to know what *they* were, what were their *kind*?

"So *what* are you?" James asked fiercely.

Jensen glanced at both Bradley and Luke, they grinned and James saw a nasty glint in their eyes as they all walked slowly towards James.

"We're *Vampires*!" they said in sync.

James gasped as they came closer. He was scared. *Very* scared.

"And we're *hungry*!" Jensen snarled as they all closed in around James.

Chapter Thirteen
Evil Lurks

AS ALL THE students slept that night Master Arthur wandered around in his office. He went to his desk and took four small potion bottles from his top drawer; each contained a pink vapour. He watched them swirling around for a moment and then he carried them over to the left-hand corner of the room. He took a small silver key from his pocket and unlocked the lid; it kind of resembled a toilet seat.

As Master Arthur lifted it up he stared down into the black and white vortex that was spinning around inside. Then slowly he took each of the bottles and dropped them down where they disappeared.

He closed the lid then and locked it, placing the key back in his pocket. He walked over to his desk and sat down. He let out a deep sigh as he placed his hands together as if to pray. "*Please* let them stay *good!*" he said as he gazed up towards the ceiling.

"*NOOOOOOOOOOOOOOOOOOOOOOOOOOOOOOOOOOO OOOOOOO!*"

"Drew, *what* is it!?" Rob was startled by Drew's sudden screaming in the dead of night. He got out of his bed, next to the mirror and walked over to Drew.

Drew was sat up in his bed clutching his duvet tightly as he stared ahead in horror. "Mate, are ya' *alright?*" Rob asked as he sat on Drew's bed.

Drew didn't answer, he just stared into the darkness, his heartbeat was racing.

Rob looked concerned as he waved his hand in front of Drew's face trying to get his attention and snap him out of the kind of trance he appeared to be in.

"Did ya' have a *vision?*"

Drew nodded, still staring off into space. "What was it?"

Drew shook his head; he didn't want to tell him.

"*Tell* me!" Rob insisted. Drew shook his head again.

"If ya' tell me what you saw then maybe I can help ya'!", Rob told him. Drew shook his head again for the third time.

"*Why* won't ya' tell me?" Rob asked looking worried. "Don't ya' *trust* me?" Drew didn't say anything as he turned his head away from Rob.

"I thought we were *friends?*" Rob said sounding a bit upset.

"We *are*", Drew said quietly.

"Then please *tell* me Drew", Rob asked again, "what did ya' *see*?"

Drew turned to look at him then, "I…I…", he stuttered, "I…want *Jonathan*. He *knows*, I can tell *him*. Please fetch him for me".

Rob looked at him. "I *can't*", he said shaking his head, "I *can't* get into their room, it's the dead of night anyway! Just tell *me please*".

Drew shook his head, "I want to tell *Jonathan!*" he was almost in tears.

"Well ya' *can't*, can ya'!", Rob said getting annoyed. "You don't need *them* anymore, you've got *us* now, and you're gonna have to *trust* us!" Rob shook his head and climbed back into his bed as Drew sat and stared out of the window. He looked at the full moon in the night sky, knowing that there was evil out there. Tears streamed down his face as he sat in the darkness. He didn't want to be here, he wanted to go home, for he knew that whilst he was at this Academy, his visions were getting *stronger*.

Out in the darkness, amongst the tall trees, a red cloaked figure stood, waiting patiently in the moonlight.

Another figure cloaked in black emerged from behind the trees and approached the figure in red.

"You have *news*?" the black cloaked figure said in a low gravely voice.

"Yes Master", the red-cloaked figure replied. It was a female voice. "Four new rookie's attended today, all seemed like very good *friends*".

"You think they are the *ones?*" asked the black-cloaked figure.

"Yes Master".

"You have been wrong before".

"I know, but I've been watching them. They have a *strong* bond, a *connection*, I am certain this time".

"Then you know what you must do?" the black figure grinned.

"Yes Master", the female bowed, "I'll keep an eye on them, let them settle in and then, when the time is right, I'll make my move".

The black cloaked figure grinned again. "Yes, make sure the prophecy does *not* come to pass", he said.

"Don't worry Master", she reassured, "I'll turn them *against* each other. I'll *break* that bond".

They bowed and then headed off in opposite directions.

Underneath one of the duvets in one of the dormitories of The Academy of Merlin, a student sat alone in the darkness, his red eyes glowing as he clutched a small black bowl and spoke into it.

"Yes Father", he whispered, "I have done as you wished".

He listened as the voice in the bowl spoke back to him. Only he could hear it. "Yes Father, when they leave they *will* join us. I'll round up *others* too. We can build up an *army*".

He listened again as his father spoke. "No Father, but..."

His father interrupted him, he sounded angry.

"Yes Father, I'm sorry, I *will* do it, but not until I *leave*. The rules *forbid* it". He listened anxiously as his father replied.

"Yes Father", the boy whispered, "you have my *word*".

Unbeknown to this boy, outside in the main room, a dark shadow emerged. Its arms stretched up as it took the form of a dark haired handsome man. He was dressed in a thick black jumper with black jeans; big black boots and wore a long red overcoat which flowed behind him as he walked around in the darkness.

He then stopped and glanced at the door that led to the dormitories before taking a small, round black compact mirror from his pocket. He looked at the skull on the lid before opening it up and watched as a reflection began to form in the mirror.

The reflection did not speak just stared back with narrowed red eyes as it listened to what this man had to say.

"Master, I have obeyed your wishes and watched over him all his life. I watched as he made friends with three others and followed him through the vortex. Unfortunately he did *not* enter alone, they all came *together*, and as I tried to *lure* him down the *right* path I regret to inform you that they took the *wrong* one and he now attends this Academy". He closed his eyes and held up the palm of his hand as the eyes in the mirror shone brighter, they were not happy. "Fear not though Master", the man continued as he opened his eyes, "for he has been placed in the group that we had *expected* and *hoped* for. I will keep my eyes on him and do all I can to guide him towards *evil*".

The eyes in the mirror decreased in brightness as this news pleased him.

"I promise you Master that when the time is right, you will be *reunited*. He will stand by your side and together you *will* be victorious".

The reflection slowly disappeared and the man shut the mirror. He turned to look at the door as a big grin formed on his face.

"You have no idea of *who* you are", he said, "but I'm going to *help* you".

He placed the mirror back in the pocket of his coat and raised his arms. His sturdy body began to glow as he decreased in size. He walked slowly away into the shadows, in the new form he had now taken.

About the Author

Laura Siobhân Croft lives in a small village in the UK near Spalding and started writing at a very young age. It has always been a passion of hers to write and draw out fantasy stories. At the age of 14, she created her first graphic novel series called *Sky Boarders*. In 2012, she had her first book published based on the *Sky Boarders* story. She is hoping to publish the first graphic novel of the *Sky Boarders* series, too.

Laura has always been a fan of magic and the supernatural and as a child, enjoyed watching Japanese Animé which inspired her to write and draw her own characters with their own stories.

Her biggest dream is to see her stories get turned into their own successful animated TV series. She knows with the right support and guidance, she will make that dream a reality!